FANTASTIC
STORIES

FANTASTIC STORIES......

BY ABRAM TERTZ

NORTHWESTERN UNIVERSITY PRESS
EVANSTON, ILLINOIS

NORTHWESTERN UNIVERSITY PRESS PAPERBACK EDITION
Northwestern University Press, Evanston, Illinois 60201

"You and I" and "The Icicle" translated from the Russian by Max
Hayward. "Graphomaniacs," "At the Circus," and "Tenants"
translated from the Russian by Ronald Hingley. "Pkhentz"
translated from the Russian by Manya Harari.

CONTENTS

AFTER THE DEATH of Stalin we entered upon a period of destruction and re-evaluation. It is a slow and inconsistent process, it lacks perspective, and the inertia of both past and future lie heavy on it. Today's children will scarcely be able to produce a new God, capable of inspiring humanity into the next historical cycle. Maybe He will have to be supplemented by other stakes of the Inquisition, by further "personality cults," and by new terrestrial labors, so that after many centuries a new Purpose will rise above the world. But today no one yet knows its name.

And meanwhile our art is marking time between an insufficient realism and an insufficient classicism. Since the loss it suffered, it is no longer able to fly toward the ideal and to sing the praises of our life in a sincere and elevated style, presenting what should be as what is. In our works of glorification resound ever more openly the notes of baseness and hypocrisy. The most successful writers are those who can present our achievements as truthfully as possible and our failings as tactfully, delicately, and untruthfully as possible. Any works that lean too far toward an "excessive verisimilitude"—meaning realism —fail. This is what happened with Dudintsev's novel Not by Bread Alone, *which stirred up a lot of noise and was publicly anathematized for blackening our bright socialist reality.*

But is the dream of the old, good, and honest "realism" the only heresy to which Russian literature is susceptible? Is it possible that all the lessons that we received were taught in vain and that, in the best of cases, all we wish is to return to the naturalist school and the critical tendency? Let us hope that this is not so and that our need for truth will not interfere with the work of thought and imagination.

Right now I put my hope in a phantasmagoric art, with hypotheses instead of a Purpose, an art in which the grotesque will replace realistic descriptions of ordinary life. Such an art would correspond best to the spirit of our time. May the fantastic imagery of Hoffman and Dostoyevsky, of Goya, Chagall, and Mayakovsky (the most socialist realist of all), and of many other realists and nonrealists teach us how to be truthful with the aid of the absurd and the fantastic.

—ABRAM TERTZ, *On Socialist Realism*

YOU AND I

F ROM the very first, this affair had a strange flavor. On the pretext of celebrating his silver wedding anniversary, Genrikh Ivanovich Graube invited four colleagues, including you, to his apartment, and he pressed you so hard to come that evening that it seemed as though your presence was the main object of the get-together.

"I will be mortally offended if you don't come," he said with emphasis and fixed you with his eyes, which were like convex lenses. There was an icy, hypnotic glint in them.

Realizing that you must not give away your suspicions too soon—or he would sense them and take measures that you hadn't thought of and that would certainly be even more cunning—you politely accepted. You even congratulated Graube on his bogus anniversary. His reasons for inviting you were obscure, but your heart was heavy with foreboding.

Sure enough, as soon as you came in, the guests leaped from the chairs to which they had been rooted while waiting for you to appear. Two of your colleagues—Lobzikov and Polyansky—winked at each other in delight.

"Here he is!"

"Let's begin!"

With these words they betrayed their treacherous designs, and to cover up, the host, Genrikh Ivanovich, was forced to motion them all to the table. But you gave not the slightest sign of attaching any importance to the ominous phrase "Let's begin," as though these words blurted out by Graube's henchmen had nothing suspicious about them and conveyed only an innocent invitation to eat and drink.

"Let us raise our glasses!" you shouted loudly and with all the gaiety you could muster. "Let us hope that this silver wedding will be followed by a golden one! Cheers!"

They all raised and clinked their glasses, but, in view of the circumstances, you dashed your vodka under the table at that favorable moment when the rest, rolling their eyes, were downing the stuff in honor of Genrikh Ivanovich Graube and his imaginary spouse.

Yes, the wife and hostess at this gathering was neither one thing nor the other, but an impostor. As likely as not it was a man in disguise. He had been carefully washed and made up with powder and lipstick and had now been

produced as a lady with twenty-five years of marital service. This explained the look of disgust on Graube's face
as he kissed her—or, rather, him—in full view, as a token
of conjugal bliss, on the sinewy pouted lips. There was
no sacrifice these people wouldn't make in order to lure
you into their spider's web and destroy you!

The drink alone must have cost two hundred and eighty
rubles or so, to say nothing of the roast duck, pickled
mushrooms, and sturgeon. And for dessert, they had no
doubt bought a nut cake, and biscuits of different kinds,
and the candy, even if it was only hard candy, must have
cost at least twenty-two rubles apiece. And then what about
the butter, the sugar, and the bread?

All in all they must have paid eight hundred rubles at
the very least. Or ten thousand, if you took into account
the fact that the men playing the part of women (the wives
of Lobzikov and Polyansky were also probably fakes) had
to be fixed up with dresses and perfumes of one sort or
another, even though they were in their own standard-
issue underwear—but, there again, it might have been
bought—fancy stuff with lace, to make everything look
completely natural, in case they had to get a bit flirtatious.

And all of this large sum, in the region of fifteen
thousand rubles, had been drawn from the bank, all because of you. And you were even a little proud as you
mentally added up the expense, though all the time you
remembered that things were very bad for you, if the esti-
mate had been passed and the money allocated.

The guests ate rapidly, clicking their knives and forks
and thereby communicating with each other in a secret

5

code, like Morse. "Let's begin! Let's begin!" was being tapped out by the impatient Polyansky, who long had had a grudge against you, because the head of the department, acting on higher orders, had raised your salary and not his—quite rightly, too.

And Lobzikov, whose friendship with Polyansky was based on the proverb, "One good turn deserves another," seized a large piece of duck in both hands and bit off the side to indicate that, metaphorically speaking, a similar fate was in store for you as well. On receiving this intelligence, the guests, smacking their greasy lips, tapped their knives on their plates in chorus: "You too! You too!"

But Genrikh Ivanovich Graube, who was sitting at the head of the conspirators, shook his head slightly and, with a meaningful look, took a sip from his glass, in which the remains of his drink still gleamed. This was his way of saying that they must bide their time for half an hour or so, until you were too drunk to notice what was going on.

Then Vera Ivanovna Graube—or, rather, the man made up as Vera Ivanovna—said to you in words whose meaning was crystal clear, "Why isn't our modest friend eating anything and why isn't he drinking at all?"

He said this in a high-pitched, girlish voice, as though he really were a woman. This virtuoso performance took a lot of trouble, and it was quite out of keeping with his general appearance, which was that of a heavyweight boxer.

"Ah," he went on feelingly, so that his vocal chords almost broke, "you know, I got these ducks at the Vagan-

6

kov market. Where can you find any decent food in the stores nowadays?"

At this provocative question the guests stopped chewing and stared at you, impatiently waiting for your reply. One word of sympathy, and it would all have been over. Graube's ears, sticking out like headphones on both sides, hung over the table. His eyes, like a sniper's, roved microscopically over your face. As if this wasn't enough, you suddenly felt as though somebody invisible and all-seeing was looking at you at this moment (was it through the window, from or through the wall?) and at all those present, who were sitting bolt upright in front of their plates, as though they were posing for a group photograph.

Knowing that you could not be silent, or your silence would be taken for consent, for illegal complicity in subversion, you looked unblinkingly at the sculptured bridge of Graube's nose and said as clearly and crisply as you could, "No! You are mistaken! Vera Ivanovna should not underestimate the distribution of goods in our cities and villages. Duck, chicken, even goose, and even the rarest bird in the world, the turkey, are sold in sufficient quantity in all the stores, as much as you like!"

A sigh of disappointment, yet at the same time of a certain relief, went through the room. Graube blushed and said, his nerves strained to the utmost, "Turkey's the thing . . ."

He was going to add something just as nonsensical and ambiguous, but Lobzikov made a hissing noise through

7

his broken tooth. This was the signal for a retreat. The guests looked down at their plates or at the tablecloth. And the all-seeing eye that had been watching them squinted mockingly at the luckless spies and dissolved in a yellow patch, the color of the wallpaper, as though it had never been there.

(2)

It was snowing, and the snow fell on my eyelashes, on my cap, making it even fluffier, and on the roofs. If you narrowed your eyelids, tiny snow houses appeared between them. The light of the street lamps shone through them brightly, creating an aurora borealis. It would fill the sky and then sink down and gradually melt away. My field of vision dissolved in a blinding flood, and a yellow tear, mixed with glittering snow, dropped from my eye onto my nose; the street lamps and the roofs looked like thatched cottages under their covering of snow. Whenever I caught a tear in time and wiped it away with my glove, Nature proved to me once again that the snow was still falling and would go on falling for a long time, perhaps for ages and ages. This was one of those blissful moments when nobody knows for certain what time it is, because the sky, falling down to earth as snow, could safely pass for day, on account of its brightness, and also for night— for the opposite reason. Most likely it was an early winter morning that had dragged on into evening. One wanted to lie down and sleep, burying one's head in a snowdrift, to find, on waking up, that the snow was still falling and had stopped the passage of time.

I was thrilled by the weather. If I had been a twelve-year-old boy like Zhenya, hurrying down Kirov Street with his skates under his arm, I would have thought that I was going home to a picture book and a Christmas tree with golden tinsel. A similar anticipation of secret delight was aroused in Nikolay Vasilyevich by a certain brunette, as he hurried, slightly drunk, through the cold, firmly believing that she would receive him in her well-heated room, as she had done twice before, to their mutual satisfaction. And why, he thought to himself, should there be a hitch the third time, since the cognac was already doing its work and the brunette had many secret charms of a specific nature?

Gradually, through the snowdrifts and the walls, and also through Nikolay Vasilyevich's back, which, pierced by electric light, receded down an incline toward the brunette, a panorama unfolded before me.

It was snowing. A fat woman was picking her teeth. Another fat woman was gutting a fish. A third was eating meat. Two engineers were playing a Chopin duet. Four hundred women were simultaneously giving birth in the maternity wards.

An old woman was dying.

A coin fell under a bed. A father said, laughing, "Oh, Kolya, Kolya!"

Nikolay Vasilyevich was racing through the cold. The brunette was douching in a basin in readiness for their meeting. A woman with auburn hair was putting on

9

trousers. Three miles away, her lover—also called Niko-lay Vasilyevich, for some reason—was sneaking through a bloodstained flat with a suitcase in his hands.

An old woman was dying—a different one this time.

Goodness me, the things they were doing! Cooking sago pudding. Shooting guns and missing. Unscrewing bolts and weeping. Zhenya was rubbing his cheeks, his skates pressed under his arm. A shop window was smashed. A woman with auburn hair was putting on trousers. A door-keeper spat with disgust and said, "Here they are! They've come!"

Racing with a suitcase in a basin in readiness for the meeting. Unscrewing cheeks from a gun, giving birth to an old woman and laughing: "Here they are! They've come!" A brunette was dying. Zhenya was dying and be-ing born. A girl with auburn hair was playing Chopin. And another girl with auburn hair—the seventeenth in succession—was putting on trousers.

The whole point was the synchronization of these acts, each one of which had no meaning by itself. All these people were unaware of each other and, what is more, they did not know that they were details in a picture composed by me as I looked at them. Little did they know that their every move was under observation and liable to careful investigation at any moment.

It's true that some of them were troubled by conscience, but they had no way of sensing that I was watching them all the time, directly, penetratingly, and vigilantly, never taking my eyes off them. In their ignorance they behaved very naturally, perhaps, but also most shortsightedly . . .

Suddenly my eye met an obstacle and jumped as though it had been hit. This was a man whom one could not fail to notice. In the empty, snow-swept street he attracted attention by constantly looking over his shoulder. Even indoors, surrounded by food and drink, receiving the hospitality of a kindly host, he behaved like a criminal who might be caught and unmasked at any moment.

He was in no danger of any sort and I tried to figure out what it was that gave him this foreboding of my presence. He must have caught some sharp look of mine and squirmed under it without realizing what it was all about and ascribing to the people around him a power which they didn't have. He had a hunch that he was being watched, and I *was* watching him, but he thought it was *they*. I found this very funny. I concentrated on him and took a closeup of him in the bright focus of my eye. He was like a germ under a microscope and I examined him down to the last pathetic detail.

He was ginger-haired and had a pale, delicate face of the kind that never gets sunburned, though it was dotted here and there with faded freckles which also thickly covered the backs of his hands and merged in solid patches on his fingers. He was nattily dressed, with a crease in his trousers, a new tie, and clean socks, which for a bachelor of his age was a sign of secret pride, if not of a fondness for women.

This impression, however, soon turned out to be wrong. Taking them for men, he showed no interest in the women around the table, except perhaps for Lida, the librarian, who was sitting on his right. He knew her from the Min-

11

istry library where he borrowed the journal *Kraftstoffe* and detective novels in translation, and he had every reason to believe that she really was Lida the librarian, and not an imaginary agent.

Lida was also given to fantasies and, out of the kindness of her heart and because of her youth, she never resisted any advance. Two years ago Graube had had a brief affair with her and he had now invited her to his family party, out of pity. She drank heavily and in silence, indifferent to what was going on.

This did not escape the attention of my charge. Emptying a second glass of vodka under the table, he leaned over to her and said, so that everybody could hear, "Lida, I love you!"

(3)

You had never believed in loose living. In love you liked to be straightforward, never making empty promises or giving dubious vows, but paying modest fees of twenty-five, thirty, and sometimes fifty rubles in cash in return for the innocent reward that, by mutual agreement, was due to you. Thus you were spared scandals and court costs in these matters and, although Polyansky said that his wife cost him less than a prostitute, each session working out to about fifteen rubles, you were convinced that it was better to pay too much than to be miserable for the rest of your life.

And if you were ever short of money, you could go for a month, or even a whole year, without getting involved with the Ministry typists. Invite one of them to the movies and you'd have no end of trouble later on just for one lousy little pinch above the knee. You could never tell with an honest woman whether she would give in or not, and this uncertainty was always disturbing and demoralizing. If only they would say "No!" right away and leave.

And so when you bent over to Lida and suddenly began to make advances, it was the result of an extreme emergency. You had parried Graube's first attack with dignity, but you felt that he was still one up on you. At any moment there would be another offensive and you had to get in first at all costs.

It often happens that an elderly man, a solid citizen (say, a member of the Academy), comes to a party, drinks a couple of glasses, and, before you know where you are, he is stuffing the silver into his pocket, reciting dirty limericks, or sitting under the table and refusing to surface again. Behavior of this kind is always treated with indulgence. Well, that is, he'll get a bawling out, people will laugh at him—"What do you mean, Vasya, you son of a bitch, dragging the honor of your uniform on the floor and casting a shadow on the Academy with your drunken puss?" But at the same time they'll slap him on the shoulder, tell him not to worry, and stick up for him. All this because he is obviously one of them, didn't go to a smart school before the Revolution, and is as morally pure as Jesus Christ. A chap like that would never divulge a military secret or betray his country at a critical moment. He is immediately cleared of all suspicion and he has nothing in the world to worry about.

This was a situation that made you envious, and you were trying to attain it with the help of Lida, the librarian, the only woman who could save your reputation. Finding her at your side, only a foot away from you, you exclaimed in sudden inspiration, "Lida, I love you!"

The spies looked at each other in consternation, and Lida, not believing her ears, sat motionless. Her forlorn collarbones protruded above her flat décolleté breast. Her raised elbow looked like a duck's wing that had been picked clean.

"Lida, I love you!" you said again even more loudly and clasped her leg just above the knee with your limp hand.

"Not in front of all these people," Lida whispered and gratefully stroked the hand squeezing her leg. And so began your love affair, in the midst of your game with death, in full view of your persecutors, who were quite annoyed by your sudden display of temperament.

You quickly put on a show of hectic activity. You grabbed the nicest tidbits from under the noses of the other guests and shouting, "This is for you!" you ostentatiously offered them to Lida, building up a barricade of food all around her. At the same time you shouted words of endearment at her: "Lidikins! Liddlikins! Liddle-diddle-kiddlikins!" Out of the corners of your eyes you observed that all this was having some effect.

"We didn't know you were such a lad," said the spy who looked like a boxer and was playing the part of

Graube's wife, with a forced laugh. "We always thought you were such a quiet fellow who kept to himself."

He had been very much shaken in all his calculations and suspicions, but he kept up his pretense of being Graube's wife.

"Nothing of the kind, Vera Ivanovna!" you answered hotly. "What have I to hide? Who is there to hide from? I can tell you everything quite frankly: I'm an incredible ladykiller, particularly when I've had a little too much."

By way of proving the truth of these words, you went up close to him with a drunken stagger and, overcoming your natural shyness, you carefully touched the brown-and-orange-spotted camouflage that had been attached to his breast. Just as you thought: it was simply an inflated rubber cushion.

"Oh, you are a one!" squealed the frightened spy, throwing himself back in his chair, probably to prevent a complete exposure of his true function. And, swaying from side to side, you returned to Lida and gently bit her elbow so that she wouldn't be jealous.

"Not in front of all these people," she whispered in embarrassment. "Let's go outside for a while, if you really must . . ."

Graube had turned green with misery over the failure of his provocation. Now he would certainly have to pay all the silver-wedding expenses out of his own pocket.

"This is an insult!" he shouted to Lobzikov and Polyansky with feigned indignation.

Swaying like metronomes, they shook with silent laughter.

"The passion of the man! No, really, what passion!" raved the boxer who called himself Vera Ivanovna.

At this moment you had another brilliant idea: to take advantage of the scandal and run off with Lida on the pretext of uncontrollable emotion. It happens, after all— an outburst of passion, the atavistic call, sexual competition, Sigmund Freud, Stefan Zweig, and all that.

Just as drunks do when they want to pick a quarrel, you waved your arms at the company and said, "Lida, I am taking you away. Let's get out of here. Let them go on gossiping without me. It'll be easier for them to run down the ducks provided by the state. What do they think I am? I'm all right, I'm loyal. But you, Genrikh Ivanovich —I can see right through you."

And you looked him straight in the eye, with the same penetrating gaze he had used on you, as though he, and not you, were a marked man.

"Yes, yes, yes! I can see right through you!"

Lida obediently gathered her things together, her handbag and her lipstick. You handed her her goatskin coat, which had lost two-thirds of its fur. You slammed the door in Graube's wide-eyed face. He stood there openmouthed, evidently not having been empowered to detain you by force.

Thick snowflakes were falling and they engulfed you and Lida in their silent myriads. It was as though millions upon millions of parachutists with snow-white parachutes were dropping from the sky and seizing the hushed town by a massive air drop. Before landing, some of them

16

circled around and around, choosing the softest possible spot . . .

The snow prevented you from seeing the enemy's maneuvers. He had become so wily that he was following hard on your heels under cover of the blanket of snow. You, in your black coat, stood out a mile away, and your only cover was Lida. Graube had certainly sent experts after you to check up on what you would do when you were alone with her. He was shrewd enough not to take your lightning romance at face value and so, as you walked down the street with Lida, you carried on as before, stumbling along like a drunk and making her various proposals, even including a marriage proposal, so that all and sundry could hear.

Lida nestled up to you trustingly and, looking down at her feet, she said with sobs of joy, "Why didn't I meet you before, when I was still a girl of seventeen, but already quite mature?"

But you couldn't have cared less about either her past or her future. You accepted her as she was, drunk and in love, with the moth-eaten fur on her breast that provided handy protection for your face, made haggard by all you had gone through. And as you spoke to her of love, you thought longingly of the sweet moment when you would see her home and return to your bachelor apartment to sleep with an easy mind in your clean and empty bed.

Now and then you stopped and, pulling her around with an impatient movement, kissed her on the lips and the eyelids, half closed in bliss. And as you kissed her, you looked watchfully over her head, obligingly thrown back, into the murky distance beyond with its swirling snow and blackness.

You were under observation. But although you could not quite make out the expression in the eyes fixed on you from all sides, you were tempted to shout proudly to the whole world, "Okay, look! I'm not afraid! You can see that I'm busy making love to my Lida, and you've got nothing on me . . ."

(4)

I've been watching him now for four days and nights. For him I am like the python whose cold-blooded stare can mesmerize a rabbit. His ideas about me are utter nonsense, but, even if one takes his absurd fantasies as a starting point, I am not sure which one of us has the whip hand. We are both prisoners; we are unable to take our glazed eyes off each other. And although he can't see me, the beam of fear and hatred trained on me from under those reddish eyelashes is so strong that I want to shout, "Stop it, or I'll swallow you! I only have to shut my eyes and you'll vanish like a fly!" The contest is beginning to weary me.

"Get it into your fat head that you are alive and breathing only while I look at you. You are only you, because that is how I address you. You are only a man because you have been seen by God . . . Oh, you!"

He turned a deaf ear to all my friendly attempts at persuasion. He had his reasons for everything. For four nights running now he had not slept so as not to be caught unaware, and lay on his sofa ready for battle, in his jacket and trousers, staring into the darkness.

As a result of this intense scrutiny of the darkness, circles and spots of various colors appeared before him. They took the form of eyes: only eyes, unattached to ears or noses. Goggling, staring, squinting eyes, brown, gray and blue ones, flitted around the room, fluttering their lashes and settling on his chest when they got tired. If he got up, they took off again and hovered above his head, blinking occasionally with their wings.

The mornings brought him no rest: he felt that he was even more conspicuous in the light of day. But for me there was really no difference between day and night. No screen or blackout could rid me of him . . .

He felt particularly uncomfortable in the bathroom. Driven there by his genitals, which he disliked and was ashamed to expose to view, he covered himself with a newspaper, made faces, whistled arias, and tried to arouse my curiosity by suddenly appearing to be sunk in thought. All this with one aim: to divert my attention to the region of his face and hold it there for a time. As though I could be taken in by this sort of nonsense!

He was so nervous at the thought that I could see everything that his urine would not come, nor would the muscles of his rectum contract. I felt ashamed for him, and at the sight of all these contortions I suffered with him for his clumsiness.

If only it had been the persecution mania which some-

19

times afflicts highly gifted people with a sense of guilt and a feeling of being patently mediocre! He probably suffered from the disease known to medicine as *mania grandiosa*. The whole world had only one aim: namely, to make trouble for him personally. When he dashed out in the mornings to buy his bread and salami, he shamelessly referred everything he saw to himself.

Moscow swarmed with people in disguise. They pretended not to look at him, but they were peeping at him all the time. They passed themselves off as casual passersby and strolled along with vacant expressions, but for some reason they were all dressed in the same way and wore uniform dark cloth shoes. Others were in white smocks, looking like women ice-cream venders. Nobody ever bought anything from them.

But worst of all were the houses, those monsters with all their gaping windows . . .

"What a pleasant coincidence! . . . How are you? . . . Still in Moscow? . . . You haven't gone yet? . . . And how's the ulcer?"

You turned around. It was Graube, of course, clutching you by the shoulder just outside the "Gastronom." The day after the "silver wedding," you had asked for leave from the Ministry on the pretext of stomach trouble. Your colleagues had been told that you were going to Yalta on doctor's orders, but, of course, you were spending your leave locked up at home. Imagine the joy of the ubiquitous Graube at catching you red-handed on the street, during a brief sortie for food, when you were supposed to be in Yalta!

While you tried to think of excuses for the delay in your departure, Graube unceremoniously put his arm around your waist and pulled you off the pavement. Another five steps and you were in a courtyard—an obvious trap—which was covered for some reason with piles of yellow snow. Graube must have been given authority for this.

"I know, I know! *Cherchez la femme.* No questions. We've all had a bit of fun in our day."

He danced around you, as though he wanted to bite you, and wagged his finger at you—without, however, losing his grip on his bulky ministerial briefcase.

"I just wanted to have a word with you alone, my friend. You really are a card, you know! The wife can't stop talking about it. It was great fun the other evening! What a laugh! You didn't think the old lady really meant it? She just likes to entertain visitors on roast duck, there's nothing more to it . . . I know you were only joking; I got it right away. 'I can see right through you,' you said. That was a good one! Pulling my leg, weren't you? Go down on my knees, if you like. No, it's all right, I'm joking, don't get mad at me. Just a token of esteem. I haven't hurt your feelings, have I, old pal? It's not because of Lida, is it? Forgive me, fool that I am. I'll do anything for you. Let bygones be bygones. No hard feelings, and all that. You know how it is. I'm old enough to be your father. I just got in first, like Christopher Columbus. Ahead of both Lobzikov and Polyansky. But I'm sorry, anyhow—something just came over me. We've all had a little fun in our time, but you've got your principles, I see. All that about 'seeing right through me.' Well, really, now, we can still be good friends! Honest—I'll go down on my knees, if you want. I wouldn't do it for anybody else in the world—just for you, as a token of esteem. Should I?"

Before you could figure out the meaning of these words, Graube, hat and briefcase in hand, and with a quick look over his shoulder, dropped to his knees in the snow. His great moonlike face, which had turned yellow in keeping with the surroundings, was sad and rueful.

For a moment you had a wild idea that *he* might be frightened of *you* and wanted to apologize . . .

But you were not to be taken in. You were quick to see the higher strategy that lay behind this humiliating posture. One's defenses are more easily penetrated from below. A man on his knees can grab you by the legs and throw you on your back.

So, without any more ado, you leaped aside with a shout, and, seeing the look of astonishment on Graube's face, you hit him right in the eye. You turned around in the roadway. He was sitting in the snow with his briefcase lying flat in front of him. He was holding one side of his face with his hands, but he continued to look at you out of the other eye.

"Wait! Don't go away! You're wrong, I tell you," he said, sniveling and whining. "She's all yours. There's nothing to worry about. You're younger than me. Only you have to look after your health. Just whistle, and she'll come running. Should I tell her you haven't gone to Yalta? She'll come running. Should I tell her?"

But you didn't fall for that one. Forgetting about the

salami you wanted to buy, you ran back home and locked yourself in.

(5)

Lida came to see you that evening. She rang twice, but there was no answer. Through the letter box she could see part of the hall, dimly lit and cluttered with household rubbish. A pair of legs stood at an angle. Lida recognized them by the shoes and trousers. Nothing else was visible.

"It's me—Lida! Open the door, Nikolay Vasilyevich!" she shouted joyfully into the letter box.

To her surprise, the well-known legs did not budge. They were visibly shaking, but they made no move toward her. After a decent interval, Lida rang again.

The radiators were humming. A radio was playing downstairs on the ground floor.

"Nikolay Vasilyevich! It's me—Lida! Why don't you say anything? Do you think I can't see you? You're standing over there in the corner and you've got your Czechoslovak pants on, half wool. Let me in for a minute."

A switch snapped off in the hall and the light went out. Lida hovered in front of the door, wondering what to do.

"Are you angry because you promised to marry me? Well, don't worry, that's not why I've come. I'm not worried about the formalities. Honest! Why did you put out the light, Nikolay Vasilyevich? I can still hear everything. You're standing there and sighing. You ought to

23

be ashamed of yourself! People have been telling tales about me, I suppose? Don't listen to them. I've had nothing to do with Lobzikov for the last four months. Or with Polyansky. I've thought about nobody but you, since you went on leave. I haven't even kissed anyone. Honest. I'll be true to you all my life, Nikolay Vasilyevich, if you want. I'll love you forever and ever, like a wife. I'll cook your meals, if you want."

Her eyes and her lips were glued to the door. There was silence inside. A warm and rather stuffy smell came through the narrow opening. "So you don't want to pluck the rose?" she whispered, blushing scarlet. She then put her nose to the dark slit for the last time and went away.

Only when she had gone did you dare to move your numb limbs. You were feverish and bathed in sweat. How childish it would have been to rush out at a ring of the doorbell into the bright light! A blunder like that was more than your life was worth. Thank goodness you caught yourself in time and stopped dead, so nobody could even tell you were there.

And what else could you have done? Let her in? Reveal your private life to the whole world? And with whom? With that very woman, who, as you now realized, had been put onto you by Graube's orders! At the party she had provoked you into a love affair and you nearly . . . You've got to get out of here! Get out before it's too late! Before she comes back and breaks in, claiming to be your ex-fiancée, who thinks it her duty to follow you everywhere, only because you once pinched her, in an unguarded moment, a couple of inches over the acceptable line . . .

You looked out of the window, hiding behind the casement and not switching on the light. There was no retreat. Lida was waiting down below. She had no intention of leaving you alone and she was pacing like a sentry in front of the house.

Your feet were swollen and painful inside your overheated shoes. There was a throbbing of pain in your hand, damaged by that scoundrel Graube. But worst of all was the stinging, prickly sensation of your skin. You kept wincing, tossed your head, and furiously rubbed your cheeks and forehead with the palms of your hands . . .

This wretched sight hurt my eyes. They were smarting pretty badly. I had a feeling that my eyelids were propped open with matchsticks and that both eyeballs were bleeding from scratches . . .

To give myself some relief, and also to soothe the pain caused by my observation of the man, I tried to look in a different direction and went walking along such distant streets as Maryina Roshcha and Bolshaya Olenya near Sokolniki Park. But it didn't help. Wherever I went —on foot or by trolley—the same angry eyes and the same fingers, covered with freckles and red hairs, were always there in front of me . . .

I knew well enough that the whole business might end badly. When I couldn't stand it any longer, I took a taxi and drove straight to the scene of the events.

My idea was to entice Lida from her post and thus to ease the situation. I thought I might reduce the number of eyes that he had concentrated on himself by dint of imagination. But this was not my only motive: I wanted to take my mind off things. I needed a third person to amuse me and protect me from my persecutor.

The selfless Lida was standing in the bitter cold under his darkened windows. Although we were acquainted only at second hand, as it were, I knew all her soft spots. It was only a matter of five minutes before I had got into conversation with her and invited her into a nearby café to warm up a little. I called myself by the first name that came into my head—Hypolite, I think. She agreed. She had nowhere else to go anyway.

While we were waiting for the *satsivi* and the *shashlik*, I made one or two complimentary remarks, to cheer her up a bit.

"Why do you wear a beard?" she asked flirtatiously. "To make you look more important? But it makes you look old! And beards don't suit red-haired men, anyway."

"What do you mean, red-haired!" I was horrified at the ease with which she changed colors to suit her own taste.

"But you *are* red-haired," said Lida stubbornly. "There's a reddish tint. You remind me slightly of a friend of mine . . ."

I saw no point in pursuing the subject, which was dangerous for all of us, but I did say in no uncertain terms that I couldn't stand red-haired men. Red-haired people always think they're being watched, so they get terrific ideas into their heads and don't trust anybody. But in fact nobody at all watches them, nor would anybody want to. People couldn't care less about them.

"They're very jealous people, though," said Lida boastfully, "and they have very sensitive feelings and a great understanding of everything."

I saw the drift of her thoughts only too clearly, but it was all to no avail. By the time our meal was served, her red-haired Prince Charming had progressed even further in his devastating ingenuity. Lying in the darkness with his face pressed against a pillow, he was trying as hard as he could not to think about anything at all.

"Eenie-meenie-minie-moe. Eenie-meenie-minie-moe," he was muttering with great concentration.

He thought that if he disengaged his brain by means of obvious gibberish, he would rid himself of the snoopers who were spying on him from within. Not content with setting the whole outside world against himself, he had noted within himself the signs of my secret investigation and had decided to start a battle of minds with me. "Eenie-meenie-minie-moe"— how could one get through a barrage like this? Not a hope of coming to grips with it. What did it mean, this dull and uninspired rigmarole?

I said to Lida, pouring out the cognac, "Drink, Lida. Drink, Liddikins. Let's not think about red-haired people. Don't bother your head about them and you'll feel much better. Eat your *satsivi* and *shashlik. Shashlik! Shashlik! Satsivi!*

"Eenie-meenie-minie-moe, eenie-meenie-minie-moe, eenie-meenie-minie-moe . . .

"*Satsivi! Satsivi!* Eat your *shashlik*, Lida. Nice, red-haired *shashlik. Shash-* or *shish- ? lik! Lik! Lik! Satsivi!*

But however much we tried, we could not take our minds off each other and overcome the attraction which was leading us to disaster. Moreover, neither he nor I got much help from Lida. Warming up after her third glass, she said, "I like you, Hypolite. You remind me very, very much of someone I know. He gave me nice things to eat at some friends' of mine too. Only please shave off your beard. Please, dear, for my sake! Get a razor and shave it off!"

The suggestion took my breath away. "Shut up!" I shouted at her. "Not another word about sharp instruments of any kind! Do you hear?"

At the same moment I saw him raise his head.

You raised your head, as though you were listening to our conversation, and smiled. You said to yourself: I must shave! and repeated aloud, "I must shave! Eenie-meenie, minie-moe, I must shave!" And you smiled again, the second time in all these days.

I was shaking like a leaf. I seized Lida by the hand and we ran out into the street, without finishing our cognac. Here I told her, without any more ado, that I loved her madly, passionately, and didn't want to look at anybody or think about anybody but her and that therefore she must be mine right away, right here, on the spot!

You got up and switched on the light. You screwed up your eyes.

Lida said, "But it's cold here and there are too many

28

people around. If you must, let's go to your place, unless you're married."

I dragged her along the street while you heated the water and looked for your shaving brush and razor. I had very little time left. There was nothing to do but go up somebody's front stairs. It wouldn't be all that cold on the top landing, and we were unlikely to be seen.

And suppose we were seen? What did I care? I had my own troubles, and it was up to me not to take notice of anybody! Before it was too late, I wanted to get out of this game, which might end badly, and I had no other means of escape except Lida.

I went down on my knees before her. I remembered the rule that one's defenses are most easily penetrated from below and that a man on his knees can grab you by the legs and throw you on your back.

So, in fact, it happened. Lida lovingly ruffled the hair on my bent head and I put my arms around her thin legs and pushed her against the wall. I didn't want to lay her on the floor, in case she caught a cold.

I was not ashamed of my intentions, which were frank enough. After all, I wasn't doing all this for my own pleasure; I had no choice.

It would have been better if you had been in my place. The thing that you had always lacked most of all was frankness. Yet in the arms of a woman even the most secretive and arrogant of men are forced to behave naturally. Perhaps, if you had not got rid of Lida, this would have been some help to you and—who knows?—if you had been a little more trusting, perhaps you would have understood me a little better . . .

But you had decided on a different course and now the razor was clutched between your freckled fingers and you were drawing it over your cheeks, as though you really did mean to tidy them up. Seeing through your trick I was in a hurry. I had to plunge at once into what I was doing, so that you would at last cease to notice me and give up the struggle with all your furtive dreams of vengeance.

Lida was sighing deeply and stroking my hair with her eyes shut. "Kolya, Kolenka! Nikolay Vasilyevich! My darling little ginger-head! My angel!" she said over and over again.

I was not jealous, but I was upset by this constant reminder of you, by this awkward proximity to you at a moment when I was hoping to hide well away from you. I was getting dangerously close to you, and I could already see your eyes somewhere next to me. They were dilated with fury. Stop! Stop! It was too late. I entered into your brain, into your fevered mind; and your last secrets, which I had no desire to know, were laid before me. You jumped up from the table. All the witnesses of your crime gathered together. Aha! Caught you! You lunged at me, at Lida, and at the whole world, with your open razor.

"Stop! How dare you! What are you doing?"

I closed my eyes. And at once I regained the calm I had not known for a long time. Everything was dark and quiet. I could no longer see you. You no longer ex-

isted. When I opened my eyes, Lida was putting on lipstick. She was straightening her coat and her dress. She
had lost a button, and it rolled down from step to step. She
went and picked it up. Then she went down to another
floor.

"Where are you going, Lida?" I asked out of polite-
ness, rather than from genuine curiosity. There was no
answer. She was hurrying back to the beat she had left
an hour before. Looking in that direction, I saw that she
could have saved herself the trouble. There was nobody to
waylay. Our friend was sprawled under the table with
his face in lather and his throat cut. As he fell, he had
managed to smash the table lamp. The room was in darkness.

I sat down on a step until Lida had gone. But she
could not completely evade my view. I then got up and,
leaving the hospitable stairway, I set off on my usual
round through the town.

Nothing had changed. It was snowing and the time of
day was just as vague. The two engineers—his former
colleagues, Lobzikov and Polyansky—were playing Chopin. Four hundred women were still giving birth every
minute. Vera Ivanovna was applying a compress to
Graube's black eye. An auburn-haired girl was putting
on trousers. The brunette, bent over a basin, was preparing for her meeting with Nikolay Vasilyevich, who, as had
happened before, was running, slightly drunk, through the
cold. The body of Nikolay Vasilyevich was lying in the
locked room. Lida paced up and down like a sentry under

his window. I saw all this and could not get him out of my mind. I was rather sad.

You have gone and I am left. I do not regret your death. I am sorry I can't forget you.

1961

THE ICICLE

AUTHOR'S NOTE

I WRITE this story as a castaway tells of his distress. Sitting
on a piece of wreckage, or stranded on a desert island, he
throws a bottle with a letter into the stormy sea, in the
hope that the waves and the wind will carry it to people
who will read it and learn the truth long after its poor
author is dead.

But the question is: Will the bottle ever reach its destination? Will a sailor haul it up by the neck with his strong
hand and will he shed tears of pity on the deck of his ship?
Or will the seal gradually be corroded by brine, the paper
eaten away, and the unknown bottle, filled with bitter sea
water, dash against a reef and come to rest, motionless, on
the bottom of the ocean?

My task is even more difficult. Though I have no scientific or literary experience, I want my work to be printed and accorded recognition. Only in this roundabout way can I hope to reach you, Vasily. Oh, Vasily! Believe me when I say that I want, not money or honors, but only your understanding. I need no readers except you, though my story will pass through many hands, perhaps, before it happens to come your way.

What else can I do? The sea of life is vast, and the bottle is such a tiny thing, and it will have to drift thousands of miles before it reaches its destination.

Forgive me, Vasily! I do not have your address. I do not even know your surname; I had no time to ask, and when I thought of it, it was too late. But I know that, like me, you live adrift in the waves of space and time, and I hope that someday you may go into a second-hand bookshop and happen to see my battered book on the shelf.

Will you remember me? Will your heart miss a beat, and will the shadowy images of the past come to life? Will you stretch out a hand of friendship and help?

Vasily, I ask only one favor: Find Natasha. You see, she must live somewhere quite close to you. Don't be surprised that she also is called Natasha, though she is completely different from the other Natasha. But I think that their names happen to be the same. Would you believe it, she is also called Natasha! And if you don't recognize her from my description, I hope that your heart will tell you who I mean . . .

So I beg you, Vasily, find Natasha and marry her as soon as possible, while you're still alive, before it's too late. Marry her without fail, even though she may be older than you and already have children—and I believe you have a family too. But never mind. Leave your wife and marry Natasha, as I tell you. You see, this is the only chance of meeting her, and if we let it go by, we shall again lose sight of each other . . .

Don't frown, Vasily. I shall explain everything in a moment. I shall put it all down just as it happened and I shall try to do a good job of writing. Let's hope it comes out in a big printing—it's more likely to reach you that way. It's all right, you needn't worry—I've read a lot of novels and stories and I have a fair idea of how it's done. And the main thing is that I have the time. If it comes to that, what's to stop me from becoming a famous writer during the rest of my long life?

And, as you follow the story, Vasily, keep a close watch on yourself. Perhaps something will stir in you and you will help the wretched castaway . . . And, as you sit with Natasha in some beautiful arbor, you will take her sadly by the waist and say, in the words of the poet:

> Do not sing, my beauty,
> Songs of sad Georgia:
> They bring to mind
> Another life and a far shore.
> Your cruel songs, alas,
> Bring back the steppe at night
> And the face of a poor girl
> Far away in the moonlight.
> Seeing you, I forget

37

The dear, doomed wraith,
But you sing, and once again
I picture it before me.

Incidentally, this was written by the Pushkin you know so well. But you were wrong when you said that Pushkin was shot. He was killed in a duel, by a pistol. I know this for a fact, believe me.

One more thing: should you read my tale of woe to Natasha? Much better read her Pushkin, and love her as I loved her. And be happy.

This is all I ask of you.

✿✿✿✿✿✿✿

NATASHA and I were sitting on a bench on Tsvetnoy Boulevard. We were quite alone. It was icy underfoot and no one ventured out onto the boulevard except Natasha and me—because we were in love and were not worried about falling and hurting ourselves.

"Disgusting!" I said. "It's enough to drive you mad. If the weather doesn't change by tomorrow, and if we don't have snow, I shall refuse to see the New Year in. Have you ever known anything like it at the end of December? . . . Nor have I. It's all these atomic tests and the arms race. Cold in summer and rain in winter. We've had it."

I was going to develop my idea about fallout in the

atmosphere, as a result of which there would be a new Ice Age and we would all grow shaggy hair and start breeding mammoths, but Natasha interrupted me. She said that in her early childhood she had once seen it snow in the middle of June. This, she assured me, had happened when they were vacationing in the country near Saratov in 1928.

This tale struck me as absolutely fantastic. It was all quite impossible, for the simple reason that Natasha was then only two and could not have remembered her snowfall. Our memory has a limited capacity. And then there was a lot of detail about insects, butterflies, and Grandmother . . .

"Don't pull my leg," I said angrily. "Or have you been deceiving me about your age? I bet you were born in 'twenty-three, not in 'twenty-six."

I said this just to tease her, of course. I was a little annoyed because I thought that I knew her inside out. We had been friends long enough, and by this time we had told each other everything we remembered about ourselves, including things one normally tries not to remember and talk about. Although we were not married yet and were not living together, it was a whole year now since I had got her to leave Boris for good, and I met her every day or every other day. And now I suddenly learned that Natasha's life was more eventful than I had supposed. Before she had learned to walk, for example, she had been playing with matches and had set her hair on fire, and it had burned with a yellow flame—all of which she remembered well.

I was older than she, more intelligent and more widely read, and I was not one to give any points away. So I started an argument with her about vague recollections and pressed her all the harder as my chances of winning diminished.

"Now, I remember . . ." she kept on saying.

"Well, so do I . . ." I replied.

And I rummaged in my childhood memories, hoping to turn up something long since forgotten. This was probably the psychological cause of the physical changes which came over me that evening and which were shortly to alter the whole of our lives.

Now, many years later, I find it difficult to say exactly how it happened. Perhaps I had been prepared for it by the course of my previous development, and had been predestined, as they say, to go through all the things that I subsequently underwent. I don't know, I don't know . . . At that moment, at any rate, I was not thinking about this at all, but was simply battering at the gates of memory, trying to force them open and remember the past. Then some fateful barrier suddenly gave way and I hurtled headlong into an abyss with an almost physical —and unpleasant—sensation of falling. I fell down and down and down, at a loss to understand what was going on, and when I came to, all my surroundings were different and I was not quite the same.

I was in a long ravine which was hemmed in by ranges of bare mountains and flat-topped hills. The bottom was covered with a crust of ice. Trees, also bare, grew along the edge of the ice at the foot of the sheer cliffs. There

41

were not many of them, but the hollow moan of the wind showed that the forest was not far away. There was a smell of corpses. Rotten branches glowed in large numbers—though they probably were not rotten branches but bits of the moon which had been torn to pieces by wolves and which was now waiting for the moment when its bones would again grow white, luminous flesh and it would rise into the sky to the envious baying of the wolves . . .

But before I had a chance to wonder about the meaning of all this, I was charged by a monster with a gaping mouth. It moved its unseen legs at enormous speed and I guessed that it had not four, or even five, legs but at least as many as the fingers and toes on my hands and feet. Smaller than a mammoth, it was nevertheless as hefty as the largest bear, and when it was close up, I could see that it had a transparent belly, like a fish's bladder, in which tiny humans, swallowed alive, were tossing up and down in the most terrible way. The monster must have been so greedy that it swallowed its victims without chewing them and they went straight to its stomach, still writhing and jumping.

Of course, I am only giving a rough idea, in my own words, of what I felt. At the time, there were no words at all in my head, only conditioned reflexes and various religious throwbacks, as they are now called, and, in my terror, I muttered vows of such a nature that I can't bring myself to put them down on paper.

But I remember that, at that moment, these nonsensical vows had a definite effect, and the monster relented, moving off along the cliffs without touching me, and throwing up, by way of warning, a shower of electric sparks. I suppose it is only because these sparks appeared to my clouded mind as "electric" that I realized I had been passed by a harmless trolley car and I was restored to my lost sense of the actual moment.

As it now appeared, I was still sitting quietly on the bench with Natasha, who, as calm as ever at my side, had noticed nothing, and the big city, blanketed by the night, was roaring and moaning like a storm-stricken forest.

"If the weather doesn't change," I said, feeling oddly ill-at-ease, "and if it doesn't snow tomorrow, I shall refuse to see the New Year in."

But I risked no more exploration of my brain. I had been terribly shaken by this trick that my memory had played on me. Trying to keep calm and not to worry, I silently breathed in the familiar air with its stench of gasoline fumes and shimmering haze of putrescent light from the street lamps, which faintly resembled moonlight and was undoubtedly of very real electric origin. I kept looking rather anxiously at the houses, the street lamps, the trees, and the trolley cars that every now and then scurried past the houses and the trees, and it was all so real, so like itself and unlike anything else. I also noticed a large woman who was walking on the curved ice crust of Tsvetnoy Boulevard, swaying like a ballerina as she went.

She was a good distance away from us, and it was impossible to tell her age or make out her features. But her figure, heavily built and swaying merrily, somehow suggested to me that she was an old woman who really had

at one time danced in the ballet and had even had a success with Admiral Kurbatov in the role of Odette. I had
no idea how this knowledge came to me, since I had never
seen the woman before in my life, and I imagined it was
the result of pure deduction. I had no desire to check my
hunch, but I could not rid myself of a feeling that as soon
as she reached the next but one lamppost, which she was
now approaching, the ballerina would have an accident.
To be more precise, I felt that she would slip at the very
spot foreseen by me, and I even wondered whether to
warn her, but curiosity prevented me and I watched her
progress with baited breath. And when she reached the
place and fell down, throwing her short arms up in the
air, I felt a twitch of conscience somewhere deep down,
as though I myself had given her a push.

Natasha and I ran to help her to her feet. Frightened
out of her wits, the old woman just wouldn't get up; she
kept falling down again, her wet bottom on the icy ground,
saying that she couldn't stand on her right leg because the
main bone was broken. In a fearful whisper she told us
that, as she fell, she had heard a splintering, crushing
sound. There was a smell of good port coming from her
toothless mouth.

As we struggled with this wheezing heap of flesh, the
whole situation at last became clear to me. The old woman
was obviously making herself out to be in a sorrier state
than she was. There could be no question of a right leg,
because she had lost it in an accident thirty years ago and
had it replaced, in secret, by a magnificent artificial one,
which was now the real object of her concern. I would

have sworn, however, that this remarkable contraption, built of aluminum in Berlin at the expense of Admiral Kurbatov, had not been damaged in the slightest, or even scratched, during her fall.

"Up you come now, Susanna Ivanovna, you'll get radiculitis," I said sternly to the morbid old woman, and finally, in order to have some effect, I even shouted at her. Soon, however, she was pouring out her gratitude and, reassured as to the sterling quality of German aluminum, she thanked me with typical French effusiveness. It did not strike her as odd that, although we had never met, I addressed her by name. She took it all for granted and repeated over and over again that she was happy to meet such a kind young man who no doubt remembered her from her unforgettable performance of Odette on the stage of the Mariinsky Theater in St. Petersburg.

"Ah, if only I were nineteen again!" she exclaimed, and putting the tips of her ragged gloves to her toothless mouth, she blew me a kiss. Only with great difficulty did we manage to say good-by, telling her to walk with the greatest care on her shaky legs . . .

Natasha laughed a great deal and, of course, quizzed me about how I had come to know this Susanna Ivanovna. I had to invent a vague story about some magazine or other having printed an old photograph of the ballerina when she was young and which had once made a great impression on me during my teen-age interest in the history of the Russian theater. Natasha said she was terribly jealous and with wonderful charm she tried to show it on her face. Then she played the fool and cuddled up to me

45

—she was very affectionate that evening. I did my best to reciprocate . . .

But I could not get Susanna Ivanovna out of my mind. I kept thinking that the old woman was in for some sort of trouble. No, it would have nothing to do with her legs —I was sure of that. Other ways in which she might soon die cropped up in my mind. For some reason I figured that it would happen in two months, from cancer of the womb. And my head was swarming with all kinds of other presentiments.

When we were absolutely frozen, Natasha asked how we would get back—on foot or by trolley? It took me a long time to decide. I had no worries about myself, but walking with my Natasha meant almost carrying her, rather as one carries a bagful of eggs from a shop. I tried not to think about eggs breaking.

We went by trolley; it really was very slippery.

(2)

It did in fact begin to snow a bit the next day and the pavements and roads were covered by a thin blanket of it. By nightfall one had the illusion that some sort of winter had arrived, bringing cleanliness and order, and, overcoming my indignation, I agreed to see the New Year in with Natasha and Boris at a party given by some people I didn't know. It was clear to me that Boris, as the ex-husband, had been asking her to do him this favor for some time. Natasha had been pestering me now for two weeks.

"He's all broken up, you know. It's all right for you and me, but he's in a bad way. Perhaps his only pleasure in life is seeing me now and again. Just seeing me and nothing more. He even suggested that you come with me. And it's in somebody else's place, on neutral ground. They're all strangers to each other . . ."

I couldn't see why Boris was so ready to put up with my presence. In his place I would never have done such a thing. But anyway, I couldn't care less about his feelings and I didn't want to refuse anything to Natasha—as though I already sensed that it would all soon come to an end.

"All right! To hell with your Boris and your philanthropy!" I said to Natasha about an hour before midnight. We went off to see these people we didn't know, taking a couple of bottles of wine for the sake of propriety.

As always at these hastily improvised parties, when a random assortment of people come together by chance, time dragged slowly and everyone was bored. After shouting out a few toasts and kicking up a small rumpus in honor of the New Year we all somehow collapsed and became uneasily subdued. Every one of us had probably been waiting impatiently for this moment and had been looking forward to it for a week, or even a month, and now here we all were at the festive table and it suddenly turns out that we have absolutely nothing to do and it would be far better to go home and make an early night of it. But since so many hopes had been attached to the occasion, nobody left and we all sat waiting, staring at each other with sleepy eyes as though we thought that at any moment now one of us would get up and do something to make all our dreams come true.

An exuberant and handsome man of Caucasian origin, with a rakish mustache above his sensual mouth, tried for half an hour to relieve the tedium by telling funny stories about people in mental hospitals. But when he at last realized that neither his stories, known to everyone *ad nauseam*, nor his overdone Eastern accent were provoking even the faintest of smiles, he stopped grimacing and guffawing, sank into moody silence, and pouted his red lips, which were weak and effeminate.

A test pilot was chatting with his wife, in an exaggeratedly matter-of-fact way, about things to buy for the house, as though they had no chance to discuss this topic elsewhere. For the single men there was nothing to do but smoke like fiends. The single women, who were uniformly ugly, took turns going to the bathroom, forcing Natasha and me to get up every time to let them pass between the table and the sofa.

It was a sheer waste of time for everyone except, perhaps, Boris. Huddling in a far corner, he never once took his imploring, lovelorn eyes off Natasha. It was a sickening spectacle. Natasha, sitting at my side with downcast eyes and looking like death, played up to him. I didn't try to get to the bottom of this relationship and drank glass after glass, without eating.

My drunken gaze was, willy-nilly, drawn to the Christmas tree, on which they at last lit the candles, and I asked for all the other lights in the room to be switched off, so as to give them full play. They flickered cheerfully with a wonderful spluttering noise, creating the festive atmosphere we needed; and gradually, with the exception, perhaps, of Boris, we all fell under their spell and huddled up to the tree, which was like some lavishly decorated domestic altar. For a few minutes a festive spirit settled on the house—the spirit, perhaps, which we had sought in coming here and for whose sake it is sometimes worth putting up with the company of people you neither know nor like.

But the candles gradually burned down, and my feeling of unease, which had been partly dispelled by drink and had almost completely disappeared at the sight of the tree, now came back. I watched anxiously as the candles, which had lit up cheerfully at the same time, now burned out at different intervals, and—I would have said—with different shades of expression. I suppose this depended on the length of the wick and other details of their manufacture, but, for reasons everybody will understand, I was interested and disturbed by another aspect of the business.

I don't consider myself a pessimist, but I must say in all seriousness that if one thinks closely about the essence of life, it is clear that everything ends in death. There's nothing peculiar about this, and it would even be undemocratic if any one of us were to survive and keep on living. But, of course, we would all like to, and when one thinks that even, say, a Leonardo da Vinci had to die, one feels quite helpless.

It wouldn't be so bad if there were some equality about it or if it were a matter of some iron law—if, for example, we all left this life in organized fashion: in large collective units and in a definite order, according, say, to one's age group or nationality. One nation comes to the end of its alloted span and off it goes to make way for the next one. Then, of course, everything would be much simpler and one's inevitable departure would be less upsetting and nerve-racking. On the other hand, the chief complication in one's existence, and hence its piquancy, is that you never know for certain when it will come to an end, so that you always have the possibility of going one better than the next man and outliving him—even if only by an extra month or so. It is this that gives our life its interest —its risks and fears, its cutthroat competitiveness and great variety.

And so, looking at the candles, which had changed places in my drunken mind with the assembled merry-makers, I observed their different ends with interest and suspense.

Some burned out as gaily as they had lived and even gave a generous spurt of flame, brighter than before, at the end. Others started economizing halfway through, as if they knew what was coming and hoped to put off the end as long as possible. But this didn't always help them, and an occasional thrifty wick would suddenly choke in its own wax a good two inches from the bottom.

There were others which grasped the full horror of the situation only at the very end, and began to dart from side to side in their tin holders, casting outsized reflections on the walls and ceiling, entirely using up all their vital juices and gases, and which then suffocated in their own prematurely decomposed remains, their death agony being a most unseemly spectacle.

I now understand that I made a great mistake, getting absorbed in this game of my overheated brain. But a second, and even graver, mistake, which had an effect on my existence just as irreversible as the evening on Tsvetnoy Boulevard, was that I gave in to the temptation of picking out the candle which seemed most suitable and guessing from it the length of my life and the date of my death.

And what do you think happened? While all the candles around me gradually went out, I lived on and on as a humble little flame, and when the room had gone quite dark I still went on smoldering all by myself, having outlived everybody else, much to my astonishment, by at least ten years.

Someone got up to switch on the light. But I said we should stay in the dark until the last candle had completely burned out. And, not taking my eyes off it, I counted off the years to which I was entitled: one, two, three, four, five, six . . .

Altogether, counting the age I'd already reached, I got to eighty-nine, and, as I did so, a supervisor—or it may have been an ordinary nurse—came into the almost dark room and leaned over the head of my bed.

A spark of life still smoldered in me. I was dying slowly and quietly, in full possession of my faculties, and I just couldn't make it. Other people around about were snoring and rambling quietly in their sleep. There was a smell of disinfectant and excrement, and the nurse, sitting on a hospital chair, was waiting patiently for me to release her. She was very sleepy and yawned out loud, crossing herself, scratching her head, and throwing reproachful glances at me. From time to time she checked whether I had died or not, but, well aware as I was of her good reasons for trying to hurry me up, and of my own thoughtlessness in the matter, I just hadn't the physical strength to tell her in words, or make her understand by some gesture, that she could go away. I simply looked at her apologetically and was overcome by shame—shame at still being alive and despair in the presence of this good woman, the only person left in the whole world who still had the slightest connection with me. I felt so bad that I got up, quickly blew out the candle end, and switched on the light.

My drinking companions, male and female, looked at me questioningly with bleary eyes, as though I had done them, too, some wrong and it was my duty to lighten their presence in my company. Someone, yawning, suggested a game—charades, for example, or musical chairs. And again they all gave me an impatient look, as though I were the master of ceremonies here and it all depended on me. Making comic faces, I brushed the cobwebs of fear and shame from my face.

"Listen, everybody! Listen, everybody!" I shouted and snapped my fingers like a light switch. "You are about to witness a performance by the celebrated clairvoyant and

mind reader! The past is revealed and the future is foretold! Any volunteers now?"

Of course, at first nobody believed in my gifts, and
indeed, I myself was doubtful. But when I began to fire
off facts and dates and various out-of-the-way details in
the life of the test pilot, and he said I was right every time,
they were all delighted and astonished, and, interrupting
each other constantly, bombarded me with questions.

I would look rapidly at the diagram of somebody's face
and immediately give the date of birth, amount of salary,
number of identity card, how many abortions— I preferred figures, because nowadays they tell us more about
real life than anything.

"And do you foretell the future, too?" asked a girl
student from the Institute of Light Industry.

"A bit," I said evasively. "For example, in your exam
next week you'll get top marks in Marxism-Leninism. You
needn't bother to study: you'll be asked about the Fifth
Party Congress and the fourth law of the dialectic."

She clapped her hands and said gleefully that she
would study nothing except those two questions.

"How can you know that?" asked the handsome Georgian. "Who can believe you?"

"Wait a week and check up," I said, slightly offended.

But they couldn't wait and wanted proof then and there
of my ability to foretell future events, and I suddenly had
an idea.

"All right," I said, "let's wait one minute. In a minute's
time I promise you that a bedbug will appear on the wall.

53

You see the engraving over there? A Giorgione, I think. It'll go around in a circle and crawl away to the left under the next frame . . ."

And soon, just as I had said, the bedbug appeared. It crawled out from under a sleeping Venus and, having made the promised circle, wandered on to another girl— one with a broken pitcher. The women shrieked. Somebody said that there was no bedbug—that it was only suggestion on my part. Others said that it was a trained bedbug and that I had surreptitiously let it out of my sleeve. And the skeptical Georgian Apollo said, "What of it? A bedbug is nothing at all; anybody could see that coming. Let him tell us when we'll have communism in the whole world—"

I let that one go by. The Georgian was an *agent provocateur*. Looking at him out of the corners of my eyes, I could see real female breasts growing rapidly in the space between his collarbone and his diaphragm. Soon I could clearly see his young and girlish but fully formed bosom. However, he kept his mustache and other masculine attributes which, in combination with the breasts, gave him the appearance of a true hermaphrodite.

I didn't know what to make of this at first, and I thought it might be the effect of my drunken state—I was glad of an explanation that made it possible to hope that all the odd happenings of the last few days had also been due to some harmless and simple cause. But this hope was short-lived. It was not wine and vodka drunk in large quantities, but other forces, that had taken hold of me and given me a distorted image of the surrounding world.

After the Georgian, all the other guests began to change. The outlines of their bodies and faces began to waver, reminding one of the oscillating blips on a radar screen. Each line broke up and became blurred, giving birth to dozens of breathing shapes. Many of the women grew beards; people with fair hair went dark and then bald, again grew a new crop of hair; they became covered with wrinkles and then grew young again—so young that they were like children with bandy legs, large heads, and vacant eyes. These, in their turn, began to grow; their bones set, and they became fat or thin.

Just the same, each of them kept some likeness to the original form, so it was not too difficult for me to identify them and talk with them, though I could no longer be certain about their past or future.

Up to now I had known which one of them was a thief, a bigamist, or the secret daughter of a runaway White Guardist, but at present everything was all mixed up and in flux and I had no means of knowing where one person ended and another began. When a young engineer by the name of Belchikov turned to me politely and asked me to guess the year of his birth, I almost blurted out on the spur of the moment the preposterous reply—contradicting all the laws of nature—237 B.C.!

This reply came to me involuntarily and automatically, under the influence, evidently, of the changes which had taken place in Belchikov. An ancient fireman's helmet gleamed fleetingly on his head, and under his loose-fitting worsted suit there were white sheets in which he had very unskillfully draped his large torso, leaving his legs bare

55

under the trousers. But of course it was not the trousers
but the helmet and some other more elusive features which
suggested to me that Belchikov had been born in 237 B.C.

Fortunately I didn't say this aloud. The helmet dissolved into thin air, the sheets billowed, and out stepped
a woman of great beauty, no longer all that young, but
still completely serviceable—and without drapes. I saw
immediately that she was a prostitute and also, probably,
of fairly ancient origin. She moved her whole body in-
vitingly, but I had no time to feast my eyes before the
frivolous creature disappeared, giving way to a priest—
or it may have been a eunuch. He quivered for a couple
of seconds and turned back into a prostitute, but a different one this time and less attractive than the first one.
And so it went on—monks and prostitutes changing places
and trying to outdo each other, different every time in
price and quality, until at last they achieved the status of
engineer Belchikov again. He was standing in front of
me, politely repeating his question.

"Can you guess when I was born, please?"

Before he had time to change from an engineer into
something else, I said quickly that he was born on March
1, 1922, in Semipalatinsk and that he shouldn't pester me
any more with silly questions—adding, for all to hear,
that his parents had kept a butcher's shop employing one
assistant in Semipalatinsk and were not, as he liked to
write on questionnaires, poor peasants. He blushed and
took fright, and in his fear he began to tremble and hastily
change shape.

All his previous transformations had seemed to take place in the past, in ancient times, or at least in no period later than 1922 A.D. Now, however, these courtesans of his carried on their activities, and austere ascetics canceled them out and expiated them, at a different and higher stage of historical development, probably foreshadowing the inner conflict in Belchikov's further evolution. Calculating the possible limits of their fleeting existences, I realized that we had come to the middle of the twenty-fourth century. But they went flitting on by, suggesting by their behavior that even in the splendid future we shall not completely rid ourselves either of the humbug of priests or of the frailty of woman, though it will all, of course, assume new social forms and be quite different in appearance . . .

I hasten to say that I am not trying to make a theory of this or to take sly digs at anybody. I am perfectly well aware that every man, even a Leonardo da Vinci, is the product of economic forces which are responsible for everything in the world. To this I would only add that the individual, the character, the personality—or even, if you like, the soul—also have no part in life and are only reflexes of our vision, like the spots we see when we press our eyeballs or look at the bright sun for a long time without blinking.

We are used to seeing people against a background of air, which looks empty and transparent, while the human figure appears to be of great firmness and density. Now, we are wrong to attribute the unvarying density and sharp-

57

ness of outline of the human silhouette, which comes out particularly well in the bright light of day, to man's inner world and to call this his "character" or "soul." In fact there is no soul, but only a gap in the air through which mutually unconnected psychic substances rush in nervous gusts, changing according to the age and the circumstances.

When I say that whores and priests occupied a prominent place in Belchikov's life, I am far from wanting to hurt the good man's feelings. I am simply pointing out a situation common to all. It wasn't the engineer Belchikov himself, but the person using his name at the moment, or rather the indefinable empty space at present filled with his substance, which at other times gave refuge to completely different and constantly changing substances. Why this happens, I don't know—perhaps to preserve some historical balance.

Anyone who looks closely into himself will easily detect the most unexpected lapses into past and future states, the urge to steal, for instance, or to kill, or to sell oneself for money. I must say that I have sometimes felt even worse impulses in this thing called the soul, and so will you, unless you cheat and abjectly shy off. The main thing is not to be hypocritical, and then you will see that you have no right to say, "He is a thief," and, "I am an engineer," because, in fact, there is no such thing as "I" and "he," and we are all thieves and prostitutes, or even worse, perhaps. If you think you are not, then you are just lucky for the time being, but we all were in the past, even if it was a thousand years ago, or we all certainly shall be in the future, as our sweet memories and bitter presentiments never cease to tell us . . .

I later got the upper hand of my art of seeing further than our nature permits. I learned to check and control myself and to treat people as if they really were confined to the strict limits of their own personalities and biographies. But at the time I felt myself surrounded, not by a score, but by at least a couple of hundred moving faces. Frightened of falling into an abyss five hundred, a thousand, or ten thousand years deep, I kept my eyes moving. The horror of Tsvetnoy Boulevard and my descent into the age of fossil trolleys, the shame and disgrace of my recent death, imposed caution, but my eyes still darted hither and yon and there was nothing that seemed stable to them, or could be taken at its face value.

And then, in search of support, I turned to Natasha, though I knew beforehand that this was wrong. Natasha, after all, was also human and she might develop a mustache, not to mention similar characteristics of an even more basic nature. I was not quite clear about the events in store for us and, to be on the safe side, I had avoided looking at her too closely, because I guessed that this was not something to be taken lightly.

All the same, trying to find a resting place for my eyes, I did look at her and was at first relieved to see no mustache, beard, or other monstrosity that might have ruined her looks. But then, her head was not quite all there. Only force of habit made me think it was, but the more I looked, the more clearly I saw that her skull was grimly missing right down to her neck and the tip of her chin. Yet her

59

body did not fall or slip down, but remained upright in the chair and her fingers straightened invisible hair, performing pirouettes in mid-air.

It was with much trouble and visual adjustment that I reconstituted Natasha's true appearance, fitting her head and face together again, just as a restorer mends a broken vase. But I didn't want to think of fragile vessels cracking and smashing to bits, if one drops them on the pavement, hits them with a lump of ice, or, say, accidentally lets fall on them a hard object from some height. In general I tried to think as little as possible about what had happened, because Natasha was too frail for all this and might once more fail to stand up to a sudden collision with my unstable consciousness.

"Let's go home, Natasha," I said quietly, feeling tired and somehow apathetic. My sense of irreparable loss was so great that I scarcely heard Boris, who suddenly spoke from his corner. "I say, sorcerer, darling of the Gods," he said with a leer, "try and guess what I was doing last Sunday between ten and eleven!"

These were the only words he spoke, and the whole of his pent-up envy, jealousy, and shame was concentrated in this question from the corner. He didn't even spare Natasha, and named the day and the hour right to her face—"last Sunday between ten and eleven"—so as to make the sneer even worse and also to try the range of my powers to the full.

Another time I would have beaten him up on the spot and probably done a lot of other silly things. I might, in temper, have given up Natasha and returned her to Boris, saying in disgust exactly what I thought of her. But now I knew more about her than he could imagine. Among all our troubles, both present and imminent, it didn't seem to me to matter very much that Natasha had been unfaithful to me from ten to eleven—half past ten, to be exact—last Sunday.

Not looking at her, or replying to Boris, I said softly and slowly, as though nothing had happened, "Let's go home, Natasha. Let's go, please."

She got up at once and walked across the room with me, putting her warm hand into mine. I was grateful for this sign of true affection. What did I care if she was sometimes unfaithful to me, giving in to the pleas and cajolery of her ex-husband? She did it out of pity and force of habit. But she loved only me, she loved me for all she was worth and while she still could. That's something to be valued in our troubled times.

In the lobby I was buttonholed by the test pilot who pressed me up against the hatrack and said he wanted my advice. He asked me in a whisper, out of earshot of his wife, when, approximately, his end would come. He was worried about whether or not to start a family, and whether it was worthwhile buying a refrigerator.

That night I had sworn never to tell anybody the date of their death, in case their sense of the romantic was impaired and they got downhearted and lost their healthy spirit of adventure. But now I had to make an exception. Death was all in a day's work for a test pilot and not an object of idle curiosity. So I told him, as man to man, that he had five and a half years to live and would then

61

be vaporized while doing a record speed in the region of the Pacific Ocean, without even realizing the technical reason for such a sudden exit.

He was enormously pleased to hear this. Five and a half years seemed a very long time to him. He hadn't reckoned with anything like this, thinking it would all happen much sooner. He could now buy a refrigerator, and enjoy himself with his wife unhindered by contraceptives. He was as pleased as Punch.

"And now own up, old man," he said hoarsely, shaking with laughter and slapping me on the shoulder. "May as well admit it, that bedbug of yours was trained, wasn't it, like you train a dog? Some leg-pull that was! Come on, let's have the secret; I won't tell anyone . . ."

This pilot readily believed me when I predicted his death in a rocket in five and a half years' time, but it was beyond his understanding that one could predict the crawling of a bedbug over a wall.

(3)

The woodcock plummeted from the birch tree as though pulled on a string. I pressed the trigger and, taking aim, saw that it was sitting on a branch, a great black cock, looking at Diana. We climbed from our horses and galloped off. Katya, in her pink bonnet, waves good-by from the veranda. "Come back safe!" Jumping into the saddle, I run down the steps and pull on my boots.

"It's time to get up, master, it'll soon be daybreak!" Nikiphor shouts into my ear.

I clasp his fat calves in my hands. "Don't leave us, for God's sake; I implore you for the sake of your son . . ."

He looks away, white with anger. "Someone might see us, ma'am." I take the scalp between my teeth and start swimming. In the middle of the river I feel sick. With my teeth still clenched, I begin to sink . . .

"Tell me, Vasily, who is Pushkin?" my wife asks at dinner.

"He was one of those ancient Russian writers, my dear. He was shot five hundred years ago."

"And who is Boldyrev?"

"Another great writer, my dear. He wrote a play called *In the Dark* and a lot of poems. He was shot two hundred years ago."

"You know everything, Vasily," says my wife with a sigh.

I fire a cannon, I shoot with a crossbow, I shoot with a catapult. They run away. We run and run, on into the town.

"Let's go to the cellar," says Bernardo. "We've got a girl. Unfortunately she's dead, but she's not gone stiff yet."

We go down. The girl is lying belly upward on the flagstones. Her skirt is pulled up over her head.

"She won't do," I say. "What will the Virgin Mary say?"

"Nothing matters to her now," replies Bernardo.

He takes a board and places it under her back. I cross

myself and lie on her first. Bernardo presses a lever with his foot. The girl rocks under me as though she were alive.

"Get a move on," says Bernardo.

"Shut up, don't disturb me," I answer and close my eyes.

"I love you, Silvia!"

"I love you, Greta!"

"I love you, Christopher!"

"I love you, Stepan Alekseyevich!"

"I love you, Vasily!"

"I love you, my kitten, my button, my oyster, my sandwich!" they say and kiss me on the lips.

Ugh!

A gadfly is beating against the window. Snow gleams in the sun. The milk is going cold in the glass. Mitya sneezes.

He sneezes once and there is a landslide in the Himalayas, the sky falls in on us and buries us together with our stretchers.

He sneezes a second time and the Church of the Holy Trinity is struck by lightning: it thunders, the barn roof is on fire, the haystacks burn.

He sneezes a third time and there is a flood; the Lutheran priest Zinovy Shwarts, mounted on a cow, ferries chairs in their dust covers.

"Mitya!" Uncle Savely says to me, putting down his Moscow *Gazette*, "if you don't stop sneezing, I shall give you a good hiding . . ."

.   .   .

I sat at home for several days, absorbed in these visions. They came in snatches, without rhyme or reason, and I was unable to sort out my different existences and arrange them in their proper sequence, in order of time. I was also intrigued, from the scientific point of view, by the absence of any connecting links between death and birth. But apparently it was not given to me to know these subterranean stages, and so the whole logic of my transformations escaped me and I couldn't see who was so intent on making a laughingstock of me. At one moment, you see, I was a Red Indian, then an Italian, and then just poor, innocent Mitya Dyatlov who for some unknown reason died at the age of eight toward the end of the thirties in the last century . . .

Only once did I get a peep behind the curtain which came down in the intervals between scenes. I was lying on a table in a bonnet and a muslin dress, in the guise of a fully fledged corpse prepared for burial. Near the table was my husband, sobbing unashamedly, and my children were standing on tiptoe, peering with horror and curiosity into my face, which had already begun to change. But at the same time, I was still alive and I was looking down at the scene from somewhere on one side, and I cried as well, and shouted at the top of my voice, telling them to wait, because I might still rally and get up. I also asked them to remove the flowers, because they made me feel sick. But they paid no attention and carried my body out of the door, feet first, as is the custom, and I ran after them down our marble staircase, shouting to them to wait. Then I lost consciousness . . .

With this torrent of memories flooding in on me I sometimes lost any clear idea of who and where I was. I began to think that I didn't exist and that I was only an infinite series of random episodes which had happened to other people before and after my time. To reassure myself of my authenticity I would creep up to the mirror and look at myself long and hard. But this worked only for a short while.

Men are so made that they never find their appearance quite convincing. When we look in a mirror, we never cease to be amazed. "Is that ghastly reflection really mine?" we ask. "It can't be!" This inability to dissociate ourselves completely from ourselves is one of the most deadly things in life, and, as one who has witnessed his own funeral and just described what it is like, I may say that my feelings at the time were just like the common experience in front of a mirror, but ten times worse. It is the feeling of protest at being carried out somewhere, when all the time you are here inside. I imagine that there is someone inside us who violently objects at every attempt to persuade him that the person he sees in front of him is none other but himself. Hold up to his nose as many mirrors as you like and, however flawless they are, the person locked up inside you will look and wave his arms.

"You must be out of your mind! Do you really think that's me?"

"Well, who is it, then?"

"No, no, no! It's not me! It's not me!" he will squeal, in the face of all the evidence.

It is only pretty women who can fearlessly sit admiring

66

themselves for hours on end. But this is because they are not given to thinking very much, and they look at themselves not through their own eyes but through the eyes of admirers and customers. Normal, intelligent people, on the other hand, stand up very badly to the ordeal by mirror. The thing is that mirrors, like death, are contrary to our nature and inspire the same fear, mistrust, and curiosity.

We can scarcely believe that a piece of glass, daubed with some filthy stuff, is capable of faithfully reproducing us in all our profundity, and so we begin to bluster, and make faces as though to express our skepticism about the apparition defiantly stuck there in front of us. "Damn you!" we say. "Beat it! Disappear! Shoo!"

The awful thing is, though, that, contrary to common sense, he also starts making faces and blows at you and mutters right back at you, "Shoo, you idiot, shoo!"

And so you don't know who to believe—him or yourself—and you worry about world problems and have doubts, and make silly faces, until at last you lose your temper with him and go away, consoled at least by the thought that he too has gone out and the question of your immortality remains open.

Try spending a couple of hours in front of a mirror and you'll see what I mean.

But my doubts were even more agonizing.

After I had stood thoughtfully for a few minutes in front of my mirror, the images of all the people who had once lived here and also looked at themselves in mirrors appeared before me. My own original image, the one I had always known, and could confirm from dozens of photographs, was driven into the background by these highly unprepossessing faces, and it now twitched and leered and squinted, rolled its eyes and snorted, lathered itself for a shave, puffed its cheeks and squeezed out pimples and blackheads, though I myself was doing nothing of the sort and was trying my hardest to keep still and serious. I had to keep a grip on myself for fear that my face would double up with its reflection as it normally did. If I started taking over these alien grimaces, I should become totally unhinged and lose my own identity. So whenever I went to the mirror, I put on a rocklike expression.

I don't know how all these experiments would have ended, if I hadn't had one encounter which showed me all the dangers of playing with these phantoms of memory now threatening my settled existence.

He was a small, brown man, old and wizened, like a bat with folded wings. To obtain a reflection of himself he was using a lump of crystal, which fragmented his tiny figure—as though it wasn't fractured enough already —into many pieces. But then I got a closeup of his head, which was bald and bony with a tight membrane of dark, tanned skin, and the lean, malignant face peered so sharply into mine that I realized he was here and could see me. Yes, I could see him and he could see me, and we froze before each other in fright and astonishment, for he too had suddenly noticed that I was looking at him, and he was no less startled than I. "My God! Was I once *that!*" was the thought that flashed through my mind, and my wet, cold forehead was touched by a burning memory of the very distant past . . .

I was in a desert with quartz all around, holding a crystal in my hand. What shall I be like in the seventy-fifth incarnation? Shall I ask? You mustn't! I will! No one will ever know . . . And I see myself—a fine, intelligent head with skin like leather . . . But what's this—white and slimy and bathed in sweat? Just like a snail. How utterly vile! A carcass dressed in rags with a rope around its neck; must have hanged himself. A monster. He's seen me. He's looking! He's looking *from there!* Can he really see me? He can, he can . . . His lips are trembling . . . and this is me, this is me! Is *that* what I shall be like?

And almost at the same time as I saw him, I saw myself in the mirror against his dark brown background. I saw myself as he had seen me in his crystal, and the memory of the impression I had then had of my present state came back in a flash—the outlandish jacket, the tie around the neck of a white, misshapen head . . . I, with my fine, leathery head, had choked with rage at this jellyfish in a jacket. I rushed away from the crystal (the mirror?) across the desert (the room?) and, falling down on the sand (the bed?), covered my face with my hands. I think he did the same with his face—whether the one like leather or the one like jelly, I just wouldn't know any more . . .

I was brought out of my absent state by Natasha. She asked with surprise, "You're sleeping? In broad daylight?

Are you ill?" These gentle words of Natasha's were meant for me, because there was nobody in the room apart from us two.

"Yes," I said, eagerly jumping from the bed. "I was sleeping. I'm quite all right and I feel fine. I'm glad you've come, I'm so glad. I love you, I love you so much." We hugged and kissed each other . . .

Natasha's visits during these days were a relief for me. She brought a badly needed dose of reality into the house. Near her I felt stronger and more sure of life, which didn't seem quite so unstable in the company of Natasha, with whom, as I firmly knew, I was madly in love. I liked to hear her stories about the professors, the exams, and people's theses (hers was on Turgenev and she was due to graduate this year). And the way she made an omelette from three eggs in five minutes and created an effect of cleanliness and comfort with a napkin, or made a chic apron out of some towel to look like a young housewife, or bit off her thread just near the needle—all this too I liked, and it gave me a feeling that everything in the world was in its right and proper place.

As before, however, I avoided looking at her too closely. It wasn't that I feared signs of a danger which could not in any case be prevented, but simply that I didn't want to make havoc of her face, as now regularly happened if I looked too hard. So I kissed her blindly, without looking at her, and when we talked I stared at the floor or out of the window.

She noticed this change in me, of course, and thought it was because I knew about her relations with Boris. But neither of us raised any awkward questions, and we both had our reasons. I briefly explained my success as a clairvoyant on New Year's Eve by saying that I had once studied *Tom Tit's* popular system of scientific experiments and party games. She didn't ask any questions. But she wanted to know more insistently than usual if I had stopped loving her because of some small thing, and I replied that nothing had changed between us, and to prove it I gave her a hug, looking at the floor or out of the window. Although it was January, there was slush on the ground outside. Icicles hung from neighboring roofs, and though the caretakers hacked them off almost every day, they grew again like mushrooms. And looking through the window at this sight, which depressed me by its inescapability, I told Natasha that we should leave as soon as possible.

Of course, I didn't say a word about the approaching nineteenth of January or about the threat hanging over us in Gnezdnikovsky Street from the top of a large ten-story building which was quite sufficient to kill one frail woman. But having thought it all out, I told Natasha that I intended to take her out of town for a holiday in the heart of the country. There were now five days to go—it was the fourteenth—and I told her that we mustn't wait any longer and would leave that day by the night train, for which I already had tickets. However, I had no tickets, nor did I have any money, so when Natasha went out to pack, I decided, for want of any other possibility, to have recourse to Boris. I figured that he wouldn't dare refuse if I descended on him suddenly and asked without any explanation for a loan of fifteen hundred against a receipt.

In fact, he refused at first, pleading poverty, but he soon changed his mind when I told him in which secret compartment of his desk, and in what denominations, he kept his money.

"So you can see right through things? You ought to be a cop," he said with an ugly leer. "Congratulations, incidentally. You remember that girl at the party? She did get top marks in Marxism. Just exactly as you said: 'the Fifth Party Congress and the fourth law of the dialectic.' And Belchikov's been kicked out of the Party—I checked. That business about the shop in Semipalatinsk turned out to be true . . ."

I was sorry about Belchikov. I didn't want to do him any harm, but at the time I simply hadn't thought of the possible consequences. I had to be careful with Boris, he was capable of any dirty trick. Right now there was a dark cloud of greenish color curling round his head—a sure sign of depression combined with spite. It enveloped his sunken cheeks and eddied around the top of his head. It looked like tobacco smoke, but Boris didn't smoke.

"Listen," he said ingratiatingly, and no longer smiling, "take the fifteen hundred, you're welcome. But what do you want Natasha for? What good is she to you? With your phenomenal gifts you can have all the women and automobiles you want, you'll be a top-ranking diplomat, an international detective—no one will get away from you. But Natasha will only be a hindrance, she'll ruin your career. She'll sleep with all and sundry. I know her. She sleeps with me. You may be a clairvoyant, but you can't see what's going on under your very nose. She comes running to me every Sunday. Imagine, right here on this sofa . . ."

And he launched into such intimate details that I asked him to stop. I threatened that otherwise I would tell him all about the illnesses from which he was going to die.

But nothing would stop him. He was choking with passion and was trying to heap shame on Natasha in order to get her back. Furthermore, he boasted terribly, grossly exaggerating in his lurid descriptions of what had or had not happened.

I must admit that I was now in no mood for accurate prediction. Without the least regard for the truth, I said the first things that came into my head and lied shamelessly—anything to shut him up. I wanted to cause the greatest pain to this puny body which dared to make love to Natasha with such spite and effrontery before my very eyes. Our words crossed like swords—or, to use a different metaphor, like pistol shots exchanged with great rapidity at a short distance.

"Right here on this sofa. Twelve positions. First we lie—"

"First you get T.B. You lose thirty pounds in four months. You're racked by coughing and hope it's bronchitis."

"Third position: she's lying on her side and I'm lying on my side—"

"They remove your ribs. Your right lung's finished. The left one has a cavity. And you've got ulcers. You can neither sit down nor stand up—"

"I stand up and she stands up and we start the—"

"Coughing and vomiting—"

"We kiss and then bite—"

"Sweating!"

"Thighs!"

"Stomach!"

"Breasts!"

"Skeleton!"

"With our backsides!"

"Backside!"

"Right here on the sofa—"

"Here on this sofa—"

"Underneath me!"

"Bedpans!"

"But I like it best when—"

"Skin and bones!"

"When we lie in the sixth position—"

"Bedsores!"

"Sixth position—"

"Bedsores! Bedsores!"

At the sixth position I finished him off. Forgetting the manliness he had just been flaunting, he stuck his fingers in his ears and shrieked like a woman, "A-a-a-a-a-a-a-a-h! A-a-a-a-a-a-a-a-a-h!"

I went on talking a little about dropsy, but he was behaving very badly, shouting and stamping his feet, and wouldn't listen to any further details about the nasty things I had predicted for him. So, without another word, I pulled out the secret drawer in his desk, counted off fifteen hundred rubles, and wrote a receipt.

Boris had quieted down. Without taking his fingers out of his ears, he watched my lips in terror. He thought that I might start up again; he looked very ill.

I pushed the receipt under his nose. It said that I would return the fifteen hundred in a month's time. He nodded his agreement in silence. He wasn't going to risk any further argument with me. I said good-by and hurried off; I felt pretty rotten as well.

I had been severely bruised in the battle with Boris. I was prepared, of course, for what he said and I could distinguish the truth from barefaced lies, but all the same it was painful to be reminded over and over again that he did the same things with her on Sundays as I did with her on weekdays. It even occurred to me for a moment that I might go away by myself and let events take their course. But the knowledge that Natasha's life hung by a thread gave me pause and cooled me down.

Making a detour, I turned into Gnezdnikovsky Street. The danger zone had been cordoned off. They were throwing melting snow from the roof of Number 10. Icy missiles struck the asphalt and sent up showers of mud and water. The pavement groaned under the impact and the cannonade echoed through the air. At the risk of getting splashed, gaping onlookers stood and marveled at the heroism of the caretakers.

But these precautions were fruitless. The icicle was well out of reach. It was still in an embryonic form, about the

75

size of a button, and, safely ensconced under the cornice, it was gathering strength for the moment when it would strike. Nobody noticed it and it was coming on nicely.

The only thing was to get as far away as possible from this infernal machine. I went to the station and bought two tickets.

One may ask whether I understood at the time how utterly hopeless the situation was, whether I realized that our efforts were scarcely less futile than those of the care-takers and that we were only preparing the way for events and helping them to keep strictly to their timetable.

The answer is no. I dismissed all such thoughts. It must have been the instinct of self-preservation which made me put up this hopeless fight. Without this, life would be im-possible.

I tried to tell myself that my fears were absurd and stupid. This wasn't a war or an epidemic, but a ridiculous icicle with one chance in a million of accidentally hitting its target. Just cross the street and everything would be all right. And, anyway, we would be a thousand miles away from here. We would sit it out beyond the Urals and come back in a month, by which time the icicle would have melted or fallen on the head of some scoundrel who happened to pass this way. If only, I thought, Boris doesn't take it into his head to denounce me and I'm not picked up at the station, and we're not forcibly prevented from getting out of town, away from this unseasonable icy weather.

I thought we would never make it. Only when the train moved off and our car jerked and glided away did I breathe freely. I asked for two sets of bedding and while Natasha unpacked her things I sat on one side, smoking and looking at her.

The car pitched and swayed, but Natasha deftly tucked the pillows into the covers with faded monograms as though she had been doing nothing else all her life. There was so much calm about these preparations, that I leaned across to her bent figure and said, "Natasha, Natasha, let's get married."

She tucked in the ends of the bedspread in her homely manner, and sat down opposite me with one leg under her. "But you know," she said, "that Boris won't give me a divorce."

"It doesn't matter," I insisted, "from now onward we'll live together just the same. We'll set up home together in good, healthy fashion. Let's regard this trip as our honeymoon. Agreed?"

She said nothing, but, to dispel all doubt, passed her soft hand over my eyes.

(4)

Train! Train with the wings of a bird! Who invented you? None but a quickwitted people could have given you birth! Although no artful craftsman of Tula or Yaroslavl, but the cunning English Stephenson, they say, contrived you for the good of the cause, you are yet mightily well fitted to our rolling Russian plain and you speed on your way, up hill and down dale, hurtling past the telegraph poles, now faster now slower, till the head spins and the eyes hurt! Yet if one looks more closely, what is it but a stove on wheels or a peasant samovar with a line of wagons in tow? An angry creature at first sight, it's really generous and kindhearted. It puffs and blows and labors up any hill you like, grunting now and then by way of warning, but when it gives that piercing, devil-may-care whistle, you know you'd better watch out, if you don't want to be flattened.

Here we are at a station. Frantic women with babies and suitcases climb under the wheels. Others, shifty-eyed and timid, in constant fear of the powers-that-be, of round-ups and fines, sell cucumbers and chicken and potatoes wrapped in bits of cloth to keep them warm and appetizing. A legless beggar in a seaman's jersey, with his cap in his teeth, trundles himself from car to car on a rough wagon. There is hot water for making tea and a buffet with candies and cakes, and a faded banner saying "First of May" which has been there since last spring. With one more minute to go, the stationmaster, stern and watchful, lean and shriveled by his service to transport, eternally at odds with the freight trains, paces the platform in his red-banded cap.

Before we know where we are, we're off again. The women and children, the banners and the suitcases, and the last house, with the last rags airing on the fence, flash by and again we race through the icy wilderness, tearing along with thudding wheels and creaking timbers, reeking sulfurous smoke, skirting suburbs and, in the words of Gogol, "outstripping other nations and states in our headlong course."

I woke up from the cold, after Yaroslavl. The car was going along at a fair clip and shook slightly. Curled up like a kitten, Natasha was sleeping. I wiped the window and, with my chin comfortably propped on my hand, looked out, from the upper berth, at the passing countryside.

We were traveling through a white, immaculate forest and, if the day before we had suffered from the Moscow slush, out here it was a real old-fashioned winter and everything was as clean and neat as in church on the eve of a major feast. The trees, caked with snow and covered with frost, were magnificent. They had the appearance of the coconut palms, fig and banana trees, which probably grow only in India or Brazil and are quite unsuitable for our niggardly climate. And seeing these riches of unknown origin suddenly lavished on us by nature, I thought of the carboniferous period in which, as science shows, Russia, no less than Brazil, had a tropical vegetation which we now burn and send up the chimney in the form of anthracite.

But I was not depressed or driven to despair by the thought of this wastage of our tree ferns and other giant Pteridophyta. Their convoluted trunks, their feathery, fan-shaped leaves, their intricate patterns of stars and rings were consumed in the engine's firebox only to be reproduced in snow on both sides of the track. They came back almost before they perished, and, although they weren't quite the same, there was something about them, something divinely hard and crystalline, which gave an indestructible fernlike quality to all these scraggly birches and pines.

In other words, if one thinks of it logically, nothing perishes in nature; all things are interconnected and leave their mark on each other, solidifying in different forms. Thus, we humans also preserve in our mobile features, in our various habits, in our mannerisms and smiles, the fixed characteristics of all those who once lived, as though in catacombs or warrens, in our convoluted souls, leaving behind the debris of their occupation.

Until quite recently this thought had sent a shudder down my spine. My pigmy self had egotistically resisted the interlopers which, without warning, had settled in my head, like lice, threatening a total breakdown of my central nervous system. But now that I was face to face with nature and its manifest order and neatness, the presence of these other beings gave me nothing but consolation and pleasure, and made me aware of my depth, strength, and inner worth. I thought about everything that came into my head as I lay on my stomach in the upper berth, weighing up my observations of life and giving them a firm philosophical foundation.

It is amazing that science has not yet discovered and given a complete logical proof of the transmigration of souls. Yet there are examples all around us. Take the obvious one of children born with six fingers. The question is: Where did the extra finger come from? Medicine has no answer. But you only have to think about it and use your brains a little to see that one of these hidden beings, who is long since dead, has decided to make himself known by seizing his chance and putting an extra finger on someone else's hand, as though to say, "Here I am! I'm sitting here and I'm fed up and, if nothing else, I want to waggle my little finger in the world!"

Then there are lunatics. What a gift of second sight they have! A fellow walks around with his nose in the air and says, "I am Julius Caesar." And nobody believes him— nobody, that is, except me. I believe him because I know that he was Julius Caesar. Well, perhaps not Caesar himself, but he has been a great military leader of some sort —only he's forgotten who, when, and in which branch of the forces . . .

But we don't have to take these extreme cases. Is there any one of us—even the most quiet, shy, and frightened comrade—who hasn't at one time or another experienced a moment of courage, inspiration, or statesmanship? Well, there you have it! Perhaps it's Clovis or Byron coming to life in us for one brief instant, but we go on living, all unaware.

Or perhaps it is Leonardo da Vinci himself!

I won't press the point about Leonardo. I'll make a concession there. I'm concerned with the principle, not with Leonardo da Vinci. It's not myself I'm worried about. I have more than enough already: Greta, Stepan Alekseyevich (the one who shot the woodcock), innocent little Mitya Dyatlov who died when he was eight years old at the end of the thirties of the last century . . . There's no end of them. All the same it would be nice, in addition to

Mitya and Greta, to have somebody, shall we say, like Byron . . . What fun it would be, damn it all, to walk down Tsvetnoy Boulevard as a diabolic Lord Byron, eying the scene with that rather unusual Byronic look!

After history, I thought of other subjects we did at school: geography, zoology . . . They say that the human embryo goes through various stages. First, it's a fish, then apparently an amphibian, and after that it gradually grows into something like an ape. What do you make of that?! So fish, and even frogs, were given some chance of jumping around and showing off their paces in my body. Only I can see that our old teacher didn't get around to telling me that these are not just abstract stages that my organism went through while it was an imbecile embryo gradually forming in my mother's womb. In those golden days I was twin and partner, as it were, to some quite specific living carp which had perhaps swum in the river Amazon eighteen million years ago. And all other fish, every one of them, found a home in my contemporaries.

This theory—the only one, perhaps, capable of satisfying a mature mind—grew up as we traveled along in the train. Inwardly fortified by this framework of impregnable arguments, I lay in my upper berth and mused about infinity, immortality, and equality. For now I was firmly convinced that none of us will ever disappear and, in the words of the song, "will never and nowhere go under." We shall simply move to other, and perhaps even more comfortable quarters, the whole lot of us together:

Mitya Dyatlov, Greta, Stepan Alekseyevich, and the fish. Only we mustn't forget to take Byron!

We shall settle inside some roomy citizen of the future and I think that he will not be indifferent to us. He will be a polite man of tact and advanced views, and the science of these progressive times to come will have told him the whole story. And so, as he sits by his window on a quiet summer evening, he will suddenly feel a restless stirring in his soul.

His breast will suddenly brim over with certain emotions and fantastic ideas will come into his tired head. At first he will be surprised and uneasy, but then he will remember about migrant souls and say, "Ah, it's you, old pal! I know who you are. How are things? Greetings to Clovis and Leonardo da Vinci!"

Hey! You there, man of the future! Listen to what I say! Don't forget to remember me on that quiet summer evening. Look, I'm smiling at you, I'm smiling in you, I'm smiling through you. How can I be dead if I breathe in every quiver of your hand?

Here I am! You think I don't exist? You think I've disappeared forever? Wait! The dead are singing in your body; dead souls are droning in your nerves. Just listen! It's like bees buzzing in a hive or the hum of telegraph wires carrying news around the world. We were people too; we also laughed and cried. So look back at us!

I want to warn you, not out of malice or envy, but only out of friendship and fellow feeling, that you too will die. And you will come to us as an equal to equals, and we shall fly on and on into unknown reaches of time and space! This I promise you . . .

Sunk in these thoughts I had quite forgotten about Natasha—or, rather, I had stopped thinking and worrying about her and remembered only subconsciously that she was next to me, unfailingly the same as she had always been for me—my lovely Natasha and no one else. And though I would have admitted in theory that there were also other beings inside her, I somehow didn't want to know about it and dismissed the thought of its possibility. My imagination, unbridled as it was, kept her as the one and only, indivisible Natasha, untouched and eternal, and it superstitiously avoided this delicate ground. Even as I mentally planned our happy life together, I fought shy of the details and tried not to go beyond the moment when Natasha would wake up and ask me to have breakfast.

How pleasant it is to eat your breakfast on a train! And whatever you do, you're on the move! Look out the window, or turn away from it, you're still traveling just the same. Read, smoke, or pick your teeth, but all the time you're going on and on, and not a moment of your life is wasted.

And all the other wonderful things about a train! The spittoons screwed to the floor, the curved door handles (you just press and it opens!), the cool, vaguely unsettling draft from the lavatory, the faint whiff of rather bitter, but well-brewed, tea!

To warm up and put myself in an even happier frame of mind I drank a glass of wine and ate something with

it. Natasha was astonished at my appetite; I ate enough
for half a dozen people.

I wasn't all that hungry but, for the first time in my life,
I felt a curious need to swallow. It wasn't so much a
matter of eating as of simply swallowing, of bolting things
down. It was as though a bunch of children, of various
ages, were eating with me, and every time I put a piece
of something down my throat, I said to myself: This is
for you, this is for me, this is for you—and this is for
me—

I tried to be absolutely fair. I even gave a dried-out
end of salami to that nasty wizened old man with the dark
skin who had for some reason taken such an instant dislike to me, and I said, "Eat that, and keep quiet!"

But I had a particular fondness, of course, for Mitya
Dyatlov, the poor orphan; he was such a playful, mis-
chievous kid. He kept asking me for some wine, but I refused, naturally, because he was still too young. And then
what do you think the little rascal did? Natasha had
laid out some candy, he caught sight of it and started
shouting for all he was worth. "Give me some! Give me
some! I want some! I want some!" I shouted in a strange,
squeaky voice like a child's and snatched three pieces
at once from the table.

Natasha laughed uneasily. But I pulled myself together and passed it off as a joke. And I punished Mitya
for his prank: I gave the candy to another youngster—
I can't say exactly which one, but it may have been my
firstborn, the primordial little oaf who had got so scared

at the meeting with the trolley on New Year's Eve. He sucked it gratefully, grunting like a baby bear.

"Natasha," I said, after a while, "do you notice anything funny about me?"

"What do you mean?" she asked and looked at me as though she thought it was I who had seen something odd about her.

"It's nothing, really . . . But don't you think I've got a bit fatter than I was?" And I drew my hands around an imaginary figure in the air to try and give an idea of the fullness inside me.

"You always start imagining things when you've had a little to drink," she said in an anxious tone of voice, and I knew she would now ask me how I felt about her.

"Do you still love me?"

"Of course I do! I still feel exactly the same about you."

"What did you say?"

"I said I still feel just the same about you," I replied irritably, sorry that I had started this conversation.

One has only to start talking or thinking about something for it to happen. I had noticed this a long time before. Perhaps my predictions come true only because there's no escaping what is known beforehand, and if we didn't know beforehand what's going to happen to us, then it simply wouldn't happen.

"Natasha," I said imploringly, "I love you, Natasha! I love you more than ever before! I will never, never leave you!"

I wanted to put my arm around her and break off the conversation with a long kiss, since we had the compartment to ourselves and could kiss as much as we liked, not worrying about anything.

"Wait," she said and wiped her lips. "Oh, if only you knew . . . I've got to tell you something."

"You don't have to tell me—I know everything. Look over there, instead, at that house we're just passing. A wonderful little house with a roof and a chimney with smoke coming out. We ought to live in a house like that. We'd go and fetch the bread and paraffin on skis. Until the children grow up, I mean. We'll have a son or a daughter—whichever we please. Personally I'm all set to be a father. I've got the same feeling inside me that I suppose pregnant women have . . ."

She didn't get my meaning and didn't even look at the house, which had now gone by. She just couldn't wait to put her mind at rest and tell me what I knew perfectly well without her owning up to it and was better left unsaid if we didn't want to have trouble. I had never reproached her and had kept my feelings of jealousy in check, even to a certain extent limiting my mind-reading powers—anything to keep her alive and well—and the least she could have done would have been to wait a little before telling me about her affair with Boris.

And what could she tell me that I didn't know already? All she said, playing it down a little, was that she had once on the spur of the moment gone farther with him than he deserved and now regretted it bitterly. But her timid, tearful words were enough to stir up my thoughts and send them off in this direction. No sooner had Boris's name been spoken than it occurred to me that he would scarcely have let us go just like that, and that people would be on our heels at any moment. The evening before, he had got moving and denounced me to the authorities, who would certainly intervene and spoil everything. The moment this thought crossed my mind I understood that unavoidable disaster was lurking somewhere close by and that I had known about it all the time, and that I had only been fooling myself by pretending that everything was all right.

"Please don't get the wrong idea," Natasha said, sobbing in my arms. "I love you and I hate Boris! But I think I'm pregnant, and I don't know who it is. Do whatever you like . . ."

God, this was really the limit! What the hell did I care about her goings-on with Boris! Who cared which one of us it was? Hadn't I been going to tell her that I was willing to take responsibility for her pregnancy, as long as she didn't talk to me about Boris and attract the attention of the four people in uniform who were now going through the train, checking people's documents?

They had evidently got on after Yaroslavl and had been gradually getting closer to us as they slowly moved through, checking up on the passengers. They were now only three cars away and, although I couldn't make out everything at such a distance, I knew well enough who they were looking for and the nature of the instructions in the breast pocket of their chief, who, for some reason, was called Sysoyev.

And there were four more men—I had only just noticed this—moving up from the other end of the train and going through the passengers with a fine-toothed comb. We were in the middle. They were closing in from both sides.

"Natasha! Stop crying! That doesn't matter at all. But tell me, why did you phone Boris just before we left? Did you tell him the number of our compartment? . . . No? Well, that's something to be thankful for."

There was no time to explain things to her. I was somehow confused and my mind wouldn't work. All my conflicting feelings—all the parasites traveling on my ticket —got into a flutter and pulled me in different directions. Some—probably those who had been women—told me to leave Natasha immediately ("Why get involved with trash like her?") and clear off while the going was good. Others were worried about the money, spent all for nothing, which had to be returned in a month. Somebody else advised me to offer armed resistance.

I couldn't make out who this was. Was it Stepan Alekseyevich with his aristocratic bravado? Or the Red Indian who had gone under with the scalp in his teeth? Or was it some soldier, as yet unidentified, buried inside me together with the cowards and the pennypinchers? Dear old unknown soldier!

Armed with his moral and physical support, I immediately choked off the shabby mob. "Shut up, you bastards, I'll hang the lot of you!" I muttered through my teeth, and when they had quieted down and stopped hissing, one could hear the rattle of the wheels and the creak of the wooden partitions which muffled the creak of boots and the distant murmur of the people who were coming through looking for me.

I then said to Natasha that we should get out of the train, but she didn't ask how—we were going along at full speed over the snowy plain—all she wanted to know was: what about the suitcases? I grabbed her by the hand and dragged her along the corridor. Luckily for us, there was nobody by the door at the end, and, as I had foreseen, it was not locked, as they usually are, to stop people from jumping out and crippling themselves. The cold wind hit us right in the face.

"Jump! Jump!" I shouted to Natasha, making myself heard above the noise of the wheels. "Snowdrifts—you won't get hurt! Honest! Jump, I'm telling you . . ."

But she was afraid to jump from such a height and at such a speed, and she didn't know that there was nothing to be afraid of here, that she was guaranteed against harm, and that, jump as much as she liked, nothing at all would happen to her. I would have jumped first, to show her the way, but I feared that if I did, she would go on without me and then I would have no way at all of helping her.

The four men in uniform were going through our car and were getting near the end of the corridor. I began to push Natasha and hit her across the hands, telling her to jump immediately, but she wouldn't listen to me and hung on with her hands; she kept saying that I shouldn't throw her out and that she no longer had anything to do with Boris.

Perhaps I would have managed to push her out and jump after her at the last moment, but the people who had been tipped off by Boris rushed us and had us surrounded in a second. They fired orders and questions at us: Who were we? What were we doing here? Why was the door open? I said we had come to get a breath of fresh air because my wife wasn't feeling very well.

Natasha was trembling all over. She couldn't get rid of an odd feeling that I had wanted to push her under the wheels of the train. However, she confirmed that we had come to get a breath of fresh air, and once again I was impressed by her character. . . . But all this was meaningless now. I had been recognized.

"You're under arrest. I must ask you to come with me," said the man called Sysoyev. He put my identity papers in his breast pocket and handed me a document which I didn't bother to read. I had a feeling all this had happened to me before, and even Sysoyev's cape, a splendid fur-lined officer's cape, seemed familiar. I had never seen Sysoyev, or his white cape, in my life, but I just knew that the whole thing would be like this; this was how I pictured it from the start.

The sad thing was that they didn't arrest Natasha as well. They told her she could go where she pleased and, saying she would return to Moscow, she began to weep for the third or fourth time that morning.

"Don't think," she said, "that I'm going back to Boris. I will wait for you. They'll let you go soon. It's a mistake, I'm sure of it. Don't think . . ."

They took us off the train at the next station. It was a dry and frosty morning. Half the passengers came running along to see who had been caught. A peasant woman in a sheepskin coat crossed herself in my direction, as though I was a corpse. The eight men in uniform escorted me proudly and respectfully, like a distinguished visitor from abroad. At least four of them were gripping the ribbed butts of the revolvers in their coat pockets.

"You can say good-by to your friend," said Sysoyev. "And as for you, lady, I suggest you rest up in the station here. The train back to Moscow doesn't go till evening."

I put my arms around Natasha and told her quietly and clearly the last thing I could at this fateful moment. "Natasha! Think what you like about me, call me a madman if you like, but remember one thing: when you get back, keep away from Gnezdnikovsky. You know the street—near Pushkin Square and Gorki Street. Don't go there on any account, and be particularly careful on Sunday, the nineteenth of January. Remember: the nineteenth—in four days' time. At ten in the morning. Stay at home. If worst comes to worst and you go to Boris's— don't shake your head; I know. The nineteenth is a Sunday and you may want to go to Boris's. Well, so what! Nothing to it, I don't mind at all. Only don't go through Gnezdnikovsky. It's quite out of your way, and you'll be late in the bargain—you're always there from ten to half past. Well, that's all right. You'll have plenty to do and time will go quickly. Stay till twelve if you like. It doesn't matter now. But whatever you do, remember: Gnezdnikovsky . . . the nineteenth . . . ten o'clock in the morning . . ."

No sooner had I told her about this thing that had been on my mind for so long than I realized I shouldn't have said it. If I hadn't told her not to, perhaps it would never have occurred to her to go there, but now I had prepared the way myself and it was too late to do anything about it.

"What Gnezdnikovsky Street?" she asked, "What are you getting at? I've never been anywhere near the place!"

I just shrugged, screwed up my eyes in pain and anger, and shouted, "Let's go!" to my escort. After fifty yards or so I looked back. Natasha was still standing there, but I couldn't see the expression on her face. Her head was cut off from me by a footbridge. But the rest of her body, from the breast downward, was visible. She had kept her figure perfectly and there was no obvious sign of any pregnancy. All I could see was a dark spot in her womb, which was as firm and pure as crystal.

What's all this about? I thought. Why doesn't this rotten seed planted by Boris grow and develop according to the laws of nature? I've said I'll adopt the child, no question of it. So why is there no little fish to wave good-by to me with its tiny fin?

But no matter how hard I looked, the spot would not grow or adopt the required shape. It was just as dark and unchanging as ever, and at last my eyes began to hurt from the effort.

"Where's the helicopter?" I asked Sysoyev, who was waiting respectfully for me to get over my grief. "You're always late, Captain Sysoyev."

"It will be here in half an hour," he said and suddenly saluted, flapping his cape.

(5)

I came into the hands of Colonel Tarasov. My acquaintance with this splendid and straightforward man began
with his spinning a closed cigarette case in the air and
barking gleefully at me, "Come on now! Look sharp! Can
you count? How many?"

Thinking that he had in mind the reproduction of Vas-
netsov's *Three Knights* engraved on the lid, I said that
there were exactly three men sitting on three horses.

"How many cigarettes, I'm asking you!" he roared and,
seeing now what sort of problem it was that interested him,
I named the number of cigarettes—I no longer remember exactly what it was—contained in the case engraved
with three knights. Having checked my ability to get my
bearings in space and to see objects through a layer five
millimeters thick, the colonel went on to experiments in-
volving time. He aimed a handy-looking Browning at my
face and asked in how many seconds I expected him to
shoot.

I found this very funny and, swaying in my chair, I
laughed and laughed until the colonel's hand had gone
numb from holding the heavy revolver and his eyes were
all bloodshot from the strain of trying to keep it trained on
my face as it went to and fro. Then I said, "In the first
place, my dear colonel, your gun is not loaded. In the
second place, you answer for my person with your life
and you wouldn't want to throw it away for a mere experi-

ment. And in the third place," I went on, "you will now put the gun back in your desk and start talking to me in a different tone. Otherwise I shall refuse the practical co-operation which you are about to suggest . . ."

The colonel looked hurt and said, "Hmm." He put the revolver in a drawer and dropped his familiar tone. Thus we became friends.

There was no point in my hiding from him my unusual psychological makeup. There was a complete list, drawn up by Boris for a lengthy report, of all the feats of clair-voyance performed by me in public on New Year's Eve. This document, checked by the interrogation of eyewit-nesses, had provided the excuse for my detention as a person "capable of rendering services in the national interest" and had come to Colonel Tarasov through the appropriate official channels for his further investigation and action.

I didn't want to set myself up as a kind of miracle man, but I thought it my duty as a citizen to help Colonel Tara-sov in his grand strategy. And I may say without false modesty that during the brief time I worked with him I did quite a bit for the benefit of the country and peace-loving mankind as a whole. For example, I deciphered a few mysterious telegrams sent by a certain foreign cor-respondent to a government-inspired newspaper abroad. I also foretold the fall of the cabinet, forty-eight hours before it happened, in a certain insignificant country and thus enabled our diplomats to make their financial over-tures in good time . . . I can't go into these matters in any great detail because of their highly secret nature. All I can say is that I made some contribution, that my work was not in vain, and that I did my bit for the cause we all have so much at heart.

At first my chief was very pleased with me, and to show his heartfelt appreciation, he said, "You'll go a long way. In a week or two, you'll see, you and I will uncover a major conspiracy. There hasn't been one now for ages. And with your help we'll finish the investigation in no time—we'll get the whole lot right away!"

This plan didn't appeal to me very much—not that I have any sympathy for plotters, but simply that all my instincts as an intellectual were against tracking people down and investigating them by means of telepathy and clairvoyance. I had always thought that in the catching of a criminal there should be some romantic—or, if you like, sporting—element. Otherwise secret service and detective work will just become a mere routine of rounding people up and thus lose all its glamour for the younger generation. Moreover, I was still very mindful of how I myself had recently been hunted down and I was not at all anxious to encourage him in these long-term ideas.

"Wait a minute, Colonel. Even my knowledge has its limits. I'm afraid spies are out. They're awfully scattered and difficult to keep track of. I should think about one in every hundred of the population is a spy. Not bad, really. Quite a small percentage."

"But just put your mind to it! Give it everything you've got! The whole country is looking to you with hope and telling you to do your duty! It feeds and clothes you—free education, kindergartens, crèches, reading rooms! Nothing's too much for the good old country, you son of a bitch! There's nothing I wouldn't do!"

The colonel's eyes were moist. He clawed at the buttons on the breast of his tunic and ground his teeth. Listening to all this, I felt quite ashamed.

I had indeed been given every amenity one could possibly dream of in prison: comfortable furniture, a lampshade with tassels, and a bathroom to myself. Four young men, none of lower rank than lieutenant, watched over me and fulfilled at the same time the functions of chambermaid, secretary, dishwasher, and barber, respectively. Special messengers were on duty night and day, ready to rush at any moment to the record office, libraries, and photographic archives in order to fetch anything that might be of the slightest help to me.

And the food was up to restaurant standard: three-course meals and liqueur with the coffee. True, there was some limitation on the cognac—only one bottle a day—but whenever Colonel Tarasov came in for a chat—not to interrogate me or pick my brains, but just to sit quietly after our labors and relax—the ration was increased. He thought, quite rightly, that cognac heightened my perceptions and brought out the best in me.

I remember the first time we sat up late over a bottle of Ararat. At midnight he called for a map of the world and asked me to do a bit of forecasting. At first everything went well. We polished off Europe. But then for some

97

reason he kept veering off southward to the mountains and beyond, past Ararat and Gibraltar. I could scarcely keep up with him and, quite confused as to the various troop movements involved, I lost track of who was fighting whom. At one moment I did manage to correct the situation by nudging the colonel's elbow, and we broke out to the seacoast.

This was on the other side of the equator, fifty years hence, and the colonel, putting his faith in some Negro reinforcements, was going to make an immediate landing in Australia!

"You must be mad! In the first place, we're not here, but over here. Take your finger away. And then, Colonel, you're forgetting about Madagascar. The Japs are there. What are you pointing here for? We can't come here, we shall lose the whole campaign! We can't, I tell you. After all, I know better than you what'll happen . . ."

He looked at me with tearful eyes and said hoarsely, "But what about Australia?"

"What's Australia got to do with it?"

"You mean we let Australia go to hell?"

"Look here now, we can't do everything at once. Australia's turn will come when there's another opening. At a higher stage of historical development . . ."

The colonel slid forward on his elbows across the table. "Can't you speed things up, old man? Just a little bit . . ."

"Speed what up?"

"Well, this development business . . . What are we waiting for? Make an effort! Come on, for my sake, as a friend, not out of duty. Please, be a pal, be a good fellow, help Australia on a bit . . ."

He was evidently confusing me with God. If I was in some degree omniscient, there was no question of my being omnipotent as well. What can I do? I know everything and can do nothing. And the more I know, the worse it is, and the fewer legitimate reasons I have for doing anything or putting my faith in anybody.

Of course, I was lucky to be with the colonel rather than one of those liberal-minded university types (you know the sort I mean: very sharp and Jews, mostly) who would have plagued the life out of me about free will and the role of the personality in history. But I've been saying for a long time and I can only emphasize once more that the personality plays no particular part at all. And how can a man have any kind of independence when everything is preordained? I have to stand up and I stand up. I have to lie down and I lie down. I don't want to, but I do. Because that is the law, that is historical inevitability. Try as much as you like to get out of it, but you'll still have to lie down in the end. And suppose I do try to get up again on the sly, all it means is that permission has been received and I'm only obeying the almighty will.

I have no control over myself, I have no more will or spirit than a stone, and in my more serene moments I have only one prayer: "Lord, hold me up and do not abandon me! Lord, I am a stone in thy hand. Gather thy strength and throw this stone with all thy might at whomsoever thou wilt . . . !"

"Very well," said the colonel, when I had revealed my

99

complete inability to control the course of events. "You don't want Australia; well, let's have New Zealand. Just two little islands. No trouble at all."

I repeated, quoting the dialectic, that we can neither improve on history nor detract from it, otherwise we would have chaos and subjective idealism.

"But we'll only make a tiny little improvement," said the colonel in a whining voice. "No one will ever notice. Come on now, what is it costing you? Be a pal . . . New Zealand! We've liberated Holland, but New Zealand can go to hell, you think?"

The dialectic was not Colonel Tarasov's strong point, but he had a great and insatiable soul. Perhaps the soul of Tamerlane, Peter the Great, or Friedrich Nietzsche—I turned over the various possibilities in my mind . . .

But on closer inspection, things turned out to be rather different. When I looked a little more carefully into the recesses of his large, heavyweight body, I saw drawn up behind him policemen of various ranks, guards, and overseers.

They went back to the most ancient civilizations and they emerged from the darkness in such strict order that at first I thought they all had the same face, but then I saw what it was: each was of a higher rank than his predecessor, as though they had been born specially for the purpose of rising by one degree during their lives. The last had been a lieutenant-colonel in the reign of Alexander the Second. This was the closest in rank to Colonel Tarasov, who thus stood at the apex of the whole evolution.

But as they entered history, Tarasov and all those before him had had to begin from the beginning, working their way up from the humblest of doorkeepers through all the consecutive stages of an age-long hierarchical development. It was not necessary to look into the future to see that this steady advance would not end with the rank of colonel, which was only a pause on the road to even greater heights.

I felt that Australia and New Zealand, not to mention other lesser objectives, must eventually yield to this irresistible urge for self-improvement, to this single-minded concentration of all effort on progress, and when Colonel Tarasov, for the second or third time before we said good night, begged for my support in the coming battle for New Zealand, I began to weaken. I promised to think about it and look for a way—with all due respect to the materialistic dialectic—of hastening the development of these islands, which are so out of touch with reality.

"But," I said, "I would also like a little help in a rather delicate matter concerning a woman I am living with, though I'm quite willing at any time to go through all the legal formalities with her."

"Have ten wives and live with them, if you like!" shouted Tarasov with such genuine warmth that I felt somehow ashamed about my little stratagem. But I put off telling him about Natasha, to allow him to consider the business more soberly after a good night's sleep. My head had also suffered a great deal from his powerful Ararat and before I got to sleep, I felt as though I was being rocked in a cradle.

That night I had a dream—the sort of dream that probably has some sort of meaning for one's life. I dreamed that I was walking along a road and ran into a military patrol in the darkness. I must have had something on my conscience (perhaps I was hiding from somebody or had escaped from somewhere), because the thought which flashed through my mind was: They've shot Pushkin and Boldyrev and now it's my turn. But before they could detain me and check my papers, I made off into the darkness, though they shouted at me to stop and even, I think, opened fire at random in my direction, not bothering, however, to chase me along the bad road.

A couple of times I tripped and fell flat on the ground, but it was all right—I got up again and went on, glad that I had successfully avoided a showdown with a military tribunal. My body glided easily past walls and fences which suggested that I was not far from home and would soon see all those I hadn't seen for so long. But instead of going home, I decided first to look in on a woman I knew, and I was soon under her window and climbing noiselessly up to the balcony without even disturbing the dog that slept downstairs.

Natasha was alone; she was reading a book by the light of a table lamp; and I remember thinking in my dream that all my fears had been for nothing, since she was here in such great shape. And I was suddenly curious about the book she was reading because at one time, before the war, I had tried to form her taste and had given her— much to my wife's annoyance—Pushkin's and Boldyrev's verse. But now she had in her lap my own very tattered

copy of an old story—I don't now remember the exact
title—which I had bought before the war to complete a
set and which was the work of an ancient author more or
less of Pushkin's time. I must reread it, can't remember it
—maybe it's of some interest— But surely Natasha isn't
still using my library, I thought, and gave a faint tap on
the window.

The window was shut, probably to stop moths, mayflies,
and various other insects from coming into the room from
the dark garden outside. Yet a few had nevertheless managed to get through, and they swarmed around the lamp,
beating their wings against the globe and depositing a
faint yellow dust on it. From time to time Natasha raised
her head from the book, shook the pages, and looked at
the window, but of course she could see nothing in the
darkness. Her gaze was full of the vacant longing of a
woman who has still not found what she wants in life, and
I was tormented by the feeling of my obligations toward
her, obligations which were as yet unfulfilled, but were
at last about to be. But as I tapped on the window I saw
that Natasha did not budge, no doubt taking my signals
for the tiresome commotion of the insects. Then, unable
to compete with the drumming of their battered wings,
I decided that this was because it was all happening in a
dream and Natasha couldn't hear my murmurings and
my sluggish scratching on the windowpane. So I put off
our meeting, climbed down from the balcony, and went
home across the garden and the grass swarming with
grasshoppers to the other end of the town.

The dog that my wife and I generally kept in its kennel

didn't bark as I came up and I wondered whether perhaps it had died while I was away and, indeed, whether the house itself was still there and the children alive and well. But everything seemed to be just the same, since there was a light on the ground floor in the kitchen, which also served as a dining room. My mother and father, Uncle Grisha, Aunt Sonya, and other relatives and friends whom I would never have expected to see in my house, were sitting there at a long empty table. It looked as though they were all waiting for me, as they sat there with their large, empty hands in front of them on the dining table. When I came in, they looked up and one of them—Uncle Grisha I think—said, "Ah, here's Vasily . . ."

What does he mean—Vasily? Who do they think I am? was the thought that went through my head, but only for a moment. Well, of course, that's right: Vasily! What am I thinking of!

All the same, there was something eerie about this family gathering, and I asked why there was no sign of my wife and children.

"Now don't you worry," said my mother.

"Are they dead or sick? Have they been taken away?"

"No, no, they're alive and at liberty and they feel fine. And Zhenya's such a big girl now; she's quite grown up . . ." She was in a hurry to put my mind at rest, but her eagerness only made me more worried.

"Where are they? Why aren't they here? Tell me!"

"They're here—not far away. They've gone to town. They'll be back soon . . ."

"It's no good, Lizaveta!" said my father and got up

from the table. "Vasily's not a child. We don't have to treat him like a baby. We've got to tell him!"

"No, no! Wait! Let him get used to it first!" said my mother excitedly.

But my father pushed her away roughly and blurted it out. "You see, Vasily, you're dead—"

They all looked down. It was only then that I noticed that I was standing there and talking with people who were dead, and I remembered: yes, of course! Mother and Father and Uncle Grisha had died ages ago, and I wanted to go back, before it was too late, to say good-by to Natasha and explain . . . But my father gripped my elbow so that it hurt and took me to one side.

"Have a cigarette," he ordered and thrust a bedraggled pack of cigarettes under my nose.

And quietly, so that nobody could hear, he went on: "Think of your mother's feelings and calm down. Don't you know you've been shot? Well, you were—a little while ago, just outside the town, on the road . . . Why do you stare? You shouldn't have bolted like that. It's your own fault."

"But what about Natasha? When shall I see Natasha?" I shouted and woke up in exasperation . . .

I still don't know what this dream meant and whether it is to be taken in some higher symbolic sense or whether it means that, under the name of Vasily, I really shall have to experience that dash in the night and the fruitless visit to Natasha, who won't hear my knocking in the late hours, because by that time I will have been shot. And what has Pushkin got to do with it? And who is Boldyrev? And what was that book borrowed from my library by Natasha? Was it really an ancient story, or was it the story I am writing now, under a rather different title, in the hope that one day we actually will meet after all?

On the other hand, there was a lot in the dream that could be explained by my state of mind at the time and by my impressions of life in prison. It may well be that in my sleeping state I had simply tried to break loose, but that my wish to do so had taken on a confused form. Or it may be that my past and future got mixed up, but I shall have to wait till the time comes before I can verify the dream in practice.

But I didn't think about it like this when it was still fresh in my mind. I was goaded by the idea that Natasha escaped me every time I stretched out my arms toward her. The next morning I continued my negotiations with the colonel, begging him to have Natasha put under arrest for her own protection—if only for twenty-four hours—preferably placing her in my cell, so we could be together as man and wife, as it were. Of course, I had to tell everything about the time and place of the threatened danger to her life—a danger which it was the plain duty of the authorities to avert.

But, as though a little abashed by our operations over the bottle of Ararat, the colonel was in an unusually sober mood.

"What is your reason," he asked, "for attaching so much importance to an insignificant icicle? Why should your Natasha be hit on the head by a lousy lump of ice? And why does it have to be the day after tomorrow, at

ten o'clock, of all times? That sort of thing doesn't happen
—I can't see any rhyme or reason in it. And you say
yourself that you managed to warn her. Why on earth
should she go to Gnezdnikovsky—and just at the very
moment when this icicle is going to fall on her?"

"But, Colonel, you don't understand women. She *will*
go, she will go, as sure as sure can be. Just to be annoying.
She knows she shouldn't and so she'll go. Then, why is
an icicle more insignificant than a bomb, or a germ, say,
which is even smaller to look at? Don't you see that anything accidental is quite inevitable once it's been foretold?
It's like passing sentence. You know what it's like with
your tribunals: no appeal. Some people are killed by
germs and others by icicles. And some while trying to
escape. It varies from case to case. Strictly between you
and me, we're all under sentence of death. Only we don't
know the day and the hour or the other details of the execution. But I do know, I know and I'm worried sick. If
only I didn't know!"

We argued and haggled for a whole hour before I
could get him to send in a report. He wouldn't have
Natasha arrested without the knowledge of his superiors
and he now waited for instructions. For the next two days,
however, he never left me and even had his camp bed
brought to my cell.

I also took certain measures: I had the barred window
completely covered over and all the clocks were removed
at my request. I thought it would be better like that.

We drank and worked by electric light and, quite confused as to the time of day, we would have lunch at eight

or eleven in the evening. Unfortunately I couldn't completely get rid of my sense of time and I could feel it
growing between lunch and dinner, gradually eating into
the few remaining hours left. I was also reminded of the
icicle by any sausages given us with the hors d'oeuvre.
I couldn't see it from where I was, but I could vividly
picture the icy polypus, as it gained weight like a slug,
its beak drooping down.

The most awful thing was that it was so unimpressive
in size and shape that it gave no cause for alarm. If it
had been just a little thicker and had a larger tusk it
would have been spotted and destroyed long ago. At my
request the colonel had twice sent a team of civil-defense
workers to Gnezdnikovsky, and though they searched the
whole street they could find nothing. But the icicle hung
there and preyed on my mind, while all the time Natasha
walked around freely out of my reach, and Colonel Tarasov's report went slowly from office to office without any
visible result. In other words, it was the usual story of
muddle.

Later on I often asked myself what would have happened if the colonel, in infringement of discipline, had
made a decision on his own hook and ordered Natasha to
be put in a safe place. What would the icicle have done
then? Altogether, the whole thing was a sheer absurdity,
a chain of comic circumstances each one of which was
in principle avoidable. And my gift of second sight, which
was the cause of all our troubles, wasn't that some sort of
mistake as well? If I hadn't quarreled that time on Tsvetnoy Boulevard with Natasha about snow, if the weather

had been different, then none of this would have happened. But now it was all working out exactly as it was, and I was sitting here under lock and key, waiting for the end almost with impatience: get it over and done with, come on, fall! Fall and put me out of my misery!

I was tortured by the thought that Nature in her cruelty, not content with the execution itself, would as a final touch make me a spectator of the scene which had been brought about by my own prediction, as though to say: There you are! See what a good and accurate prophet you are! And suddenly, sitting comfortably in my cell, as in a nice warm movie theater, I would see Natasha toppled onto the snow by a flashing, glasslike arrow, then the caretaker's wife coming out to put sand on the spot and the crowd, reluctant to disperse, looking up with awe . . .

But it all happened differently. We were sitting hard at work when Tarasov asked, as though making a joke, "What do you think: will they make me a general? Or will I die in the same old rank?"

This was the first time he had shown any interest in what would happen to him personally, and of course I gave an encouraging reply, saying that in time he would certainly make the rank of general and perhaps something even bigger. But, answering mechanically, just to get rid of him, I started thinking about the problem seriously, and before I knew it, an obscure vista unfolded before my mind's eye . . .

I must have been carried far into the future, and skipping a number of intermediate stages, I saw an earth which you could scarcely call by that name, it was so covered with layers of ice. I should say, however, that I use the word "ice" rather in a figurative sense, for it was still not clear what they were made of, these stalactites and stalagmites sticking up all over the place like giant icicles. Perhaps they had arisen from some petrified gas or spirit that had solidified under very high pressure, and, looking at the scene, I was not even sure that I was on our planet, and not in outer space.

But by some indefinable instinct I knew with complete certainty that these shapeless objects were not made of dead matter, but were living and rational beings, artificially created and of the highest possible evolutionary type. What is more, the icicle nearest to me and the one that seemed to be in control of everything around was none other than Colonel Tarasov—except, of course, he now had a different rank and another name, and bore very little resemblance to his previous self. However, there was something in the structure and behavior of this polypus of ice—the way it filmed over with moisture, as though sweating, and then congealed in smooth, shining spirals, but, most of all, the way in which it constantly grew and developed and, in doing so, bore down on neighboring structures with its formidable spikes—in all this, I say, one sensed the erstwhile stubbornness of purpose and statesmanlike intellect of Colonel Tarasov and also the same sort of straightforward good nature.

Please don't misunderstand me by taking these words as some sort of innuendo, or as a trick intended, as you might say, to falsify the historical process with the ulterior motive of casting a shadow over our bright future.

"But look here," some suspicious reader will exclaim, "who ever heard of such a thing! A healthy man—and a state official, at that—turning into an icicle at the highest stage of development! What is one to make of it? Isn't this defamation and character-blackening?" No, it is not, I reply firmly, and there is nothing at all to be made of it, because I'm not yet clear myself how the forces that controlled Tarasov during his existence as a colonel later assumed such a strange and novel form.

If the worst comes to the worst, and to avoid misinterpretation, I am ready to withdraw what I have said and put it down to my unbalanced state of mind. On the other hand, enough time has gone by now for me to look at the question with greater calm and objectivity and I can see nothing wrong with that stalagmitic being, which, I am deeply convinced, continued on a higher plane the great mission of my chief and protector. And although Colonel Tarasov was retired long ago, without actually getting his promotion, my promise of one was not idle talk, since I had in mind a remoter prospect beyond the limits of one human life.

The gigantic icicle revealed to me then had, I am sure, no less progressive significance than a general or even a marshal, and if we had an emperor it would probably even outdo him by its intelligence and all-round development, notwithstanding its lack of those clear marks of military distinction by which we are used to identify higher authority. But one has to take account of the fact that it grew up and got its education, as I have said, in totally different historical conditions and, it may well be, on a different planet, and what here seems to us an insignificant icicle may there, for all we know, be the veritable crown of the universe. In any case Colonel Tarasov's future seemed to me at the time to be bright and full of promise and I couldn't take my eyes off his smooth, icy surface, which was constantly growing new layers . . .

"What's wrong with you, Pop-Eye?" he asked with his usual racy humor.

As soon as he said these words, the icicle disappeared, as though it had melted or fallen under the table, and in its place, behind the inkstand, his heavy, rugged figure was sitting opposite me, its same old self again. No! It wasn't the same! The fact is that the colonel had somehow faded all of a sudden and gone haggard, as though he'd put everything he had into the icicle and was now worn out and aged by several years. I would say, even, that he was unrecognizable: a tired old man in a dirty tunic with worn cuffs that had been taken in and inexpertly mended.

But he must have a wife and children somewhere, I thought, surprised that it had never before occurred to me to wonder about the family life of this man, who seemed to be completely absorbed by matters of public importance. But I was even more astonished when, in an attempt to solve this simple problem, I found I could conjure up no picture of either the wife or the children of the colonel, who all at once became a complete mystery to me, though the secret was right there in his wrinkles, flabby cheeks, and frayed cuffs.

"Why are you just staring at me like that?" he said

in a peeved voice, shivering slightly as though he felt cold.

"Tell me, Colonel, have you ever had a wife and children?" I asked, for want of something to say.

Before he could answer, a lieutenant dashed into the room and reported that the colonel was wanted urgently on the telephone. They went out quickly, both of them very agitated about something, and even forgot to close the steel door.

At other times I would have raced after them in my thoughts and would have known all about it before they did. But at the moment my mind was working badly and my head was empty, and I simply didn't want to do anything. Overwhelmed by information coming in from all sides, I had been doing too much thinking all this time and I had been at it hard enough for me to sit now for a little while in peace.

So I sat and looked around the room which until quite recently had seemed too richly furnished, but which also looked distinctly shabby and dreary now. Everywhere there were holes and dust and boot marks, and it all had the air of requisitioned stuff: a rickety plywood chair, a sofa with broken-down legs of imitation mahogany, tattered and greasy with fingermarks on the back and a brass medallion, half of it missing, with the head of a young lady whose nose had worn away—the kind of small-scale, grubby trash in our humdrum lives that speaks of a long period of neglect and decay.

All these details meant very little to me now, and, looking at some specks of dust, which would formerly have yielded goodness knows how many terrible stories, all I thought was: A speck of dust—well, who cares? Drift on, speck of dust!

When the colonel returned and haltingly told me of Natasha's death, all I asked was when it had happened.

"A quarter of an hour ago," he said and told me briefly what he had managed to gather on the telephone from his duty officer. The duty officer—or, in plain language, the police agent—had followed Natasha at some distance and had noted the exact time of the direct hit on his stopwatch: it was at ten o'clock precisely, to the minute.

The colonel was obviously upset and, as though wishing to make up for his guilt, he loudly cursed the higher authorities who for some reason hadn't acted in time, as they should have done. I hardly listened. I wanted to go back to the icicle—not the one that killed Natasha, but the other one which promised to grow up in a million years, perhaps, after our time. I don't know what my motive was—perhaps it was a belated wish to fathom the secret of this man who was so wretched, unhappy, and mysterious in his distress. I still remembered that he could be as firm and as awe-inspiring as that icicle, but I couldn't think how this happened, and in general I couldn't picture to myself either the past or the future of this aging and ungainly soldier with his lined face and frayed cuffs. I just couldn't get him into focus; there was nothing but bits and pieces—wrinkles, buttons . . .

"What are you looking at me for?" he roared, and banged his fist on the table. "You think I'm lying? You know better than I that there was nothing I could do, nothing! You can check up for yourself. It wasn't my fault. Tomorrow we'll look into—"

"No, Colonel, tomorrow we won't look into anything," I said, taking my eyes off his wrinkles. "Unfortunately I can't be of any further use. About a quarter of an hour ago, I lost all my powers of second sight. I don't even know whether you once had a wife, Colonel. I know nothing now. It's all over."

Epilogue

Well, that's the end of my story and it only remains for me to add a few words of explanation which I couldn't fit in either at the beginning or in the middle and which might be helpful to those of my readers who would like to get it all straight in their minds. But who are my readers? And who exactly am I talking to, who am I counting on in this literary exercise? I think it is mostly myself. For one thing, when you write, you have to read and reread what you've written and so I already have one reader, thank God.

"But heavens above," others will say, "you can't be doing all this just for yourself, sitting up nights, not sleeping and completely wearing yourself out!"

"Just for myself," I tell them in all frankness, "not for myself as I am now, but for myself as I shall be at some time in the future. Which means that anybody else— readers in the here and now—can easily join me if they wish. Because nobody knows who was who or who will be who. Perhaps you—yes, you—are me. So for the time being I have to take account of the general public, but later on, we shall see."

You see what's happening all around us? A man lives on and on, but suddenly—bang!—and he's dead; then other people walk around in his place until they too are senselessly destroyed. All you hear around is: bang, bang, bang! What's to be done? How can we fight back? This is where literature comes in. I am convinced that most books are letters to the future with a reminder of what happened—letters "to be called for," in the absence of an exact address, retrospective attempts to re-establish links with oneself and one's former relatives and friends, who go on living and don't realize that they are missing persons.

A man disappears and you'll never find him again. He's broken up into his component parts and lost without trace in the crowd. I must get them all back, call them together again. Hey there! Vasily! Hello, hello! Natasha! Where are you? Greta! Stepan Alekseyevich! Where are you all? Hey, Clovis! Leonardo da Vinci! Answer me!

Not a sound from any of them . . . Everything is empty and dead, as though I had never had those three extraordinary weeks, which were too crowded for my poor brain . . .

I was released from my prison one year and four months later. Colonel Tarasov tried hard for a long time to restore my lost powers. He even fired blank cartridges at me, suspecting sabotage. But it didn't work. Then they put me in a private sanitarium and treated me for eight months. I began to walk again.

My illness was due to a feeling of insecurity. I was afraid to move my legs in case I stumbled and fell. As one who had got used to knowing everything beforehand, I found it difficult to return to normal life with all its unforeseen events. If a doctor in a white cap came near me, my heart would beat violently. You see, I just didn't know whether he was going to take my pulse or hit me on the nose. Who could tell what was at the back of his mind?

After this I had the colonel again. But his bad temper was gone and he was very gloomy. They'd given him hell because of me—wasting time on an obvious charlatan and falling for anti-scientific theories. The cognac we had drunk at government expense was also held against him. The world is full of malicious people. And then, times had changed. It was now 1953 and there was a general let-up. His career was finished.

Even so, we parted good friends. He asked me to let him know if ever I regained my second sight. I was also asked to sign a statement to the effect that I would not privately engage in black magic or sorcery. I readily agreed to everything.

I was forbidden to live in the capital. I settled down in the provinces near Yaroslavl, living the life of a hermit and working as a hydraulic engineer. In two years I had knocked together the necessary sum—fifteen hundred rubles—and sent it to Boris.

The money order was returned to me. I made enquiries and found that Boris had died in February, 1954, of T.B.

117

Who would have thought it? I didn't suspect that during our last conversation I had spoken like the oracle. But even this raving nonsense had come true . . .

Now, in my retreat, I mourned his premature death. He was, after all, an old friend. We might have met some time and talked about Natasha . . . Of course, he had some hand in the business and was indirectly to blame . . . If he hadn't denounced me then, everything would have been different. But who is without guilt?

I went to Moscow a couple of times, to look for Andreyusha. But I had no luck. He must have been quite grown up by now. I probably wouldn't have recognized him as my father—I don't mean the father who appears later in my dream, in connection with Vasily, but my real, live papa. He died when I was five years old and he was also called Andrey. Oh yes! I completely forgot to mention this. It was in those days, when Natasha was still alive and we were all still in Moscow. I was on my way to Boris for the money when I ran into a two-year-old boy with his nurse. Something about him caught my eye and I bent down and asked what his name was:

"Andreyusha!" he replied with childish simplicity.

But his little blue eyes said very much more. They were the same blue, twinkling eyes that looked into my face in early childhood. The gaze of a wise old friend, who knows what's what. I even had the impression that he was winking at me.

"Daddy!" I whispered so that the nurse couldn't hear. "Daddy dear! How are you getting along? Are you all right in your new home?"

Before Andreyusha could reply, the nurse, a peasant
woman of low intelligence, snatched him up and carried
her treasure away from me. To judge by his dandy little
suit, however, and his healthy, well-fed looks, he was in
the hands of comfortably-off and cultured parents. I
never saw him again.

Quite recently, in the station café in Yaroslavl, I ran
into the test pilot I met at the New Year's Eve party.

"You're no clairvoyant—you're a bastard! Spy!
Crook!" he said, weeping drunken tears. "What do you
mean by poking your nose into other people's lives?
You've ruined me! Taken away my youth! If I hadn't
known, it would have been all right. But look at me now!
Sixty-two days to go—is that right? Is that right? . . ."

I replied coldly that I had lied to him that New Year's
Eve about the rocket's blowing up over the Pacific in five
and a half years' time. In fact, I said, nobody knows anything—he might blow up tomorrow, or possibly never.

"You're not lying again? Honest?" he asked with hope
in his voice. "Or are you just trying to calm me down?
Well, you needn't bother. Just let me have the truth!"

He was inconsistent, the test pilot, but I could understand his inner doubts. For three weeks during that mem-
orable January long ago I myself had tried not to face the
truth, until at last it caught up with me and struck me
down. And now, without it, I was in a constant torment
of uncertainty and would have given anything to learn
the whole truth, which I had then let slip, and I prayed
God for the return of my wonderful gift, which I had
used so badly.

I should have been glad of my luck and done all I could to find out more exactly what I was in the past and will be in the future, whether I will ever meet Natasha and marry her, and how to put all the scattered fragments of my life together again. But instead, I stupidly tried to run away from death, fearing it like a child, and then it came and parted us. Natasha has gone, and so has Susanna Ivanovna. Boris is dead, too, and the test pilot hasn't long to live . . .

I don't know who it was who said, "The dead shall rise again!" Well, it's true enough. They'll rise again, all right. Every day there are thousands of new people in the maternity wards. But the question is: Do they remember anything about themselves and about us, when they rise again? And do we recognize in our carefree children those who were once our wives and fathers? But if nobody is remembered or recognized, then nothing changes, and we are parted in death by screens of oblivion. Can we afford to be so forgetful?

No! Do as you please, but until things change for the better, I shall stand by the dead. One can't leave a person in this destitute state, in this final and ultimate degradation. For who is more degraded than a dead man?

I live more and more on my memories: Tsvetnoy Boulevard, Natasha, my little differences with Boris. What an odd fellow he was. Why couldn't he get along with me? And then, Colonel Tarasov. A fine, straightforward man, Colonel Tarasov. We had good times drinking together. I haven't touched a drop of liquor since Natasha died . . .

But most of all I remember two episodes. Both of them

are from the future. The first is in the hospital at night. Everybody is asleep and the nurse is dozing in her chair, and waiting for the moment when at long last I will let her go home to bed. I still have some time to go, and I am conscience-stricken at still being alive, when all the others are dead. It's disgraceful to go on living when all the others are dead. But there's nothing I can do about it . . . And then—a quite different situation—I'm standing on a balcony and beating on the lighted window, along with the moths. But again I can't get through the transparent screen to the brightly lit room inside. Natasha is alive and sits there reading a book—the very book that I have written, perhaps. And I am writing from here and trying to break in there, not knowing whether this forlorn tapping will ever be heard . . .

Will you hear it, Natasha? Will you read to the end, or will you give up halfway through and never know that I was so close? If I only knew! I don't know and I don't remember. I ought to tell her everything from the beginning. But it's no good. Any moment now she'll close the book. Wait just one second! The story isn't finished yet. I want to tell you one more thing, the last thing I have the strength for . . . Natasha, I love you. I love you, Natasha. I love you so much, so much . . .

1961

TENANTS

✿✿✿✿✿✿✿

ALAS, my dear Sergey Sergeyevich! Can there really be any comparison between you and Nikolay Nikolayevich? The very idea is absurd. You haven't got any claim to looks and, if you'll forgive the comparison, your biceps hang down just like the nipples of some skinny old bitch. And you start hitting the brandy bottle every morning so that the only wonder is where you get the money from. But Nicky—Nikolay Nikolayevich—was a young-looking man, an engineer engaged in constructing electric motors, twenty-nine years old and in his prime. Even he couldn't keep it up. He calls me into the kitchen on one occasion. "What's this, Nikodim Petrovich?" he says. "What's going on?" And he's as white as can be. Like the ceiling.

He was in a different class from you! He used to sing! Did push-ups! He'd wake up early in the morning, do all his exercises to the sound of the radio, clean his teeth with a brush, and sing the Air Force march:

> Higher higher and higher
> We soar in the sky like birds,
> And in everyone's propeller
> Our frontiers' tranquillity whirs.

Pleasant listening, though he's a tenor and I prefer a bass. Take a tip from an old man and move out of here while you're in one piece. Pick up your suitcase and beat it. Would you like me to write a note for you as a token of friendship? To Shestopalov himself in the City Housing Department . . . Never heard of him? . . . Shestopalov. Fellow who arbitrates housing problems. I worked under him for thirteen years. In charge of a students' hostel and two apartment houses, I was. Director, manager—call me what you like. Kept it up till I got my pension. Over on the Ordynka they were: one five stories, the other six. He can track down any kind of accommodation in five minutes . . . Quite all right, I assure you! . . . It'll be on my recommendation! . . .

You'll settle down in your new place. We'll leave your library here for the time being. I'll look after it. I'll do some reading if you'll let me. I guess you haven't got *A Young Boer from the Transvaal?* Thing I read before the war, but I've forgotten the author's name. Some sort of foreigner, a Frenchman.

Ah, it's a great pity. The nights are long and my legs are aching. Rheumatic joints. Had it a long time; it's a chronic complaint . . . What's that? . . . Yes, pour away, do—it won't do any harm.

Your health!

Hmm, yes . . . you've certainly got a choice little cognac here, just what the doctor ordered. Sort of caresses the gullet. We'll both be drunkards together . . . No, no, don't bother, I don't like eating when I drink—ruins the taste. Seriously, Sergey Sergeyevich, move to another apartment. Here, I tell you confidentially—you won't like it when you find out, but it'll be too late. Really, why go on and on saying, "I won't leave, I won't leave"? It's pure laziness on your part and nothing else. Look, I'll tell you what, I'll follow you and we'll set up house together. If you don't want to get involved with Shestopalov you can arrange an exchange. Let's advertise. Together my room and yours add up to thirty-one square meters. Enough to swap for a self-contained apartment. How about it?

I'll create the right environment for you as a writer. See that things are quiet and neat—need a little peace myself. Maybe you can still manage to get married and we'll breed grandchildren and kittens. I'll do the baby-sitting, be a grandfather to them. We'll put all thought of cognac out of our minds except perhaps on the major holidays, New Year's and the First of May. We'll have an organized household. A table, a cupboard—everything as neat and clean as if we were Germans, and we'll buy me some new felt boots. That'll be the life! Let's have a drink, shall we? Your health, Sergey Sergeyevich.

Why was it, to speak frankly, that I became friendly with him—with Nicky, that is? He was a good fellow, domesticated, and kept the place in good shape. As soon as he got home from work he'd start some job. He'd run up a set of shelves with a fret saw or assemble a radio out of odds and ends, all with his own hands. And I took a liking to his Ninochka too, at the beginning. As busy as a little bee she was, kept getting things for the home. They hadn't been here six months when, believe it or not, they bought a new wardrobe. With a full-length mirror on the door. They hung lace curtains. It was all done on twenty-five or thirty rubles at a time on payday, so you might say they put their home together on kopecks. And the whole thing went to rack and ruin. Poor old Nicky! Where are you now, and who now kisses your fingers? . . . Ah, me! In a mental home, or, as people used to say, in the madhouse. But can that be called a true home? No, it's an illusion—no home but a hostel for madmen and nothing more . . .

What's that? How did it start? It all began with a mere trifle. One evening he was eating pea soup and he suddenly fished out of the plate—can you imagine such a thing?— some woman's hair. An ordinary tuft of female hair, that's all—"combings," as they call it in the country. He of course turned to his Ninochka and asked her fairly calmly what was the meaning of this. She turned all red and said, also fairly calmly, "Nicky dear," she says, "it's that Krovatkina who puts her hair in our saucepan instead of meat."

Incidentally, the hair was gray. Gray . . .

Sh-sh! So what I'm asking you, Sergey Sergeyevich, is whether you haven't got that interesting book of Fenimore Cooper's, *The Last of the Mohicans.* Yes! *The Last of the Mohicans!* About South American Indians! Yes, that's it! So you haven't! So you haven't! What rainy weather! I said, the weather's rainy! . . .

She's gone away . . . That's who it is, Krovatkina in person. A real witch. Glues her ear to the door and keeps a check on our conversation. Oh, I can sense her all right; I know. If I say so, that means I know! I've got a feeling for those things, wasn't born yesterday. I can divine their intrigues with my back. At ten yards' distance.

What's that? What do you mean, "tricks"? If you don't believe me I can prove it. All right, I'll turn my back to you now so I can't see anything, and I'll still be able to guess. Any movement you make.

Oh dear me! My legs feel as if they belonged to someone else. All right then, begin.

Here we go. At this very moment you're picking your nose. With your little finger. Now you've stopped. You've seized your left ear. You're sticking out your lower lip. Well, did I guess right? Tee-hee! And you're quite a joker! What a pantomime you played behind my back! Thinks I won't find out. Sticks his tongue out, frowns . . . And you've gone completely squint-eyed, my dear Sergey Sergeyevich. You're tight. This brew has prostrated you.

Well, that'll do for today. I can do better than this. And

now let's have a nightcap and go to bed. It's late. What will the neighbors think?

No, no. Don't even ask me. I'll tell you the rest some other time. That Krovatkina's put me off. Spoiled my mood. Rather let me perform some farewell trick. What do you say, would you like me to disappear now without leaving the spot? I'll simply slip away. One, two, three! Here I am now—here!—I am not!

Good night, Sergey Sergeyevich.

(2)

And soon only water nymphs were left. And even they— well, you know yourself—the industrialization of natural resources. Make way for technology! Streams, rivers, and lakes began to smell of chemical substances. Methyl- hydrate, toluene. Fishes simply died and floated belly up- ward. As for the water nymphs, they'd pop out and some- how cough up all that river water, and there'd be tears (believe it or not) of grief and despair in their eyes. Seen it myself. The whole of their voluptuous bosoms covered with ringworm, eczema, and (if you'll forgive my saying so) signs of recurrent venereal disease.

Where could they hide?

They didn't pause long for thought, but took the same route as the wood spirits and witches—to the town, to the capital city. Along the Moscow-Volga Canal, over those —what do you call 'em?—lock gates into the water-supply network where it's cleaner and there's more to eat. Farewell, O native land, our primordial element!

What a lot of them perished! Countless numbers. Not entirely, of course—after all, they are immortal beings. Nothing to be done about that. But the brawnier specimens got stuck in the water mains. You've probably heard it yourself. You turn on the kitchen tap, and out of it come sobs, various splashings, and curses. Have you thought whose antics these are? The voices are those of water nymphs. They get stuck in a washbasin and it's murder the way they sneeze!

Incidentally, there's a former water nymph living in our apartment, as freely and easily as could be. According to her identity card she's a Sofya Frantsevna Vinter. You know her, of course. Runs around in a fustian robe and does aquatic exercises from morning till evening. She'll splash around for three hours on end in the bathroom (so that the other tenants have nowhere to wash their hands) or sit half in a basin and sing a verse about the Lorelei. In German:

> *Ich weiss nicht was soll es bedeuten,*
> *Dass ich so traurig bin . . .*

Written by Heinrich Heine. I told her yesterday, "Sophy! You might at least show some respect for the new tenant. He is a writer, when all's said and done. And you run around the corridor in only a robe without buttons or sashes, and every time you move it flies open a couple of feet."

But she only grins, the shameless bitch. "Your writer,"

131

says she, "gave me some White Lilac. Some sort of perfume. He and I had an understanding the first time we
set eyes on each other."

Watch out, Sergey Sergeyevich. For heaven's sake don't
run after her; she'll tickle you to death. And as far as
anything more serious is concerned, I'll tell you this—
she's got fish's blood and everything else about her is
fishy. She just looks like a woman so as to lead people
astray . . .

Here you are laughing again and disbelieving everything. And though you're a writer, you haven't got any
powers of observation. Well, what can you say, for example, about Anchutker? Your next-door neighbor. Anchutker. The fellow behind this wall here. Nothing special. Just an ordinary citizen, except that he's a Jew, a
Moisey Yekhelevich. Well, I must say! If I'm not mistaken Karl Marx was also of Jewish origin.

But what if you take a real close look at him? . . .
What about his hair style? Have you ever seen wool like
that on a man's head in your life? And what about his
complexion? Where can you find another man with such
a dark blue skin? And he has a somber expression and
wears size forty-seven boots, and what's more they're
always mixed up—the right one on the left foot and the
left on the right. Goes around like that, the uncouth bear,
both at home and in the ministry.

Another point, you just pay attention to the literature
he reads. Korolenko's *Rustling Forest.* Leonov's new
novel, *The Russian Forest.* A remarkable novel, I don't
deny it. But I ask you, why does it have to be on that par-

ticular subject? And why does he work in the department of forestry, this accursed Anchutker? Counts silver
birches and fir trees on a slide rule and transfers cubic
feet around . . . He's not an Anchutker at all if you
look at it in a correct, scientific way, but an *anchutka,*
which is a dialect word for "wood devil." Get it now?
My point precisely.

No, Sergey Sergeyevich, you won't find a single living
person among our tenants. Even though they're related
to me, come from the same village, so to speak. But why
go into that? It's more than my reputation's worth. It's
just the talk of ignoramuses, of illiterate, uncultured peasant women that a house spirit is, as they say, much the
same as a wood spirit. You're wrong! They're quite different professions. It's impossible to ignore the differences
of principle involved in this problem. The house spirit is
used to a house, to the smell of humanity, to the warmth.
Has been since the beginning of time. He hasn't anything
to do with devils and witches. Perhaps you think they
share a common nature. Don't say it! There's all kinds of
nature. For example, man has also sprung from the ape.
But he later took his own path and became an independent
species. He has dealings with apes only in Africa and in
the zoo. So what do you think it's like for me, an elderly—
so to speak—person, to live on a communal basis?

When they moved into our apartment—Nikolay Niko-
leyevich and Ninochka, that is—I told them at once:
"Nicky," I said. "Ninochka! Keep your ears open. Don't
give in to provocation. Keep your distance. And I'll warm
myself at your hearth in my old age."

"No!" Ninochka answered. "When in Rome, do as the Romans do. I won't forget what happened with that Krovatkina and the pea soup. She steals our meat, and am I supposed to chew her hair? What's more, it's dirty and gray. You could catch an infection from it."

And she tells her Nicky to fit steel padlocks on all the saucepans, the point being to lock up the food while it was being cooked unsupervised on the communal stove. Sometimes she'd steal up on tiptoe, quickly unlock a saucepan, add some salt or butter, and lock it up again.

Only this didn't do any good. The strange happenings continued. She'd put on a chicken, say, to cook and snap the padlocks. But when she opened it she'd find a dead cat cooked in chicken broth. Hadn't even been skinned, there it was, fur and tail and all.

Ninochka took umbrage. Meanwhile another neighbor, Avdotya Vasyutkina, had won her over, and an alliance was formed. Avdotya had an account of her own to settle with Krovatkina. They couldn't agree how to share Anchutker. Both of them had children by him, little wood sprites, that is. And so the two enemies were battling for their witches' love.

Can you imagine the scene? A fearful commotion in the kitchen. In the smoke these witches are swaying to and fro, gripping each other's disheveled locks. They spit in each other's faces at close quarters. They call each other rude names very succinctly.

"Witch! Whore!"

"Same to you! Where did you ride off to tonight on the lavatory pan?"

Beneath their feet their blue-bellied children dodge around, trying to bite the opposing side in the calf. They're still small, but they've got sharp teeth and claws.

And Ninochka's there too—can you imagine it? Her hair's flying in all directions and her eyes are blazing like the bulbs of a pocket flashlight. She's holding a rolling pin and through her torn blouse you can see her little chicken's ribs heaving away like nobody's business.

The first time I saw this scene I burst into tears. How could an old fellow like me cope with three enraged women? I run around imploring them. "Shoo!" I shout. "Get to your corners! Or else I'll call the police." They won't even listen. The whole place resounds with groans, trampling feet, and the thunder of frying pans. Then there's that water nymph Sophy giving peals of hysterical laughter in the bathroom.

In the evening I tell Nikolay a thing or two. "Restrain your Ninochka. This business will end badly, as you'll see. Take down her woolen drawers without ceremony and let her have a few strokes of the birch to teach her not to intervene in other people's battles."

Can you believe it, he actually took offense. "I'll take it to the Supreme Soviet," he says. "I won't leave things as they are. Krovatkina should be taken to court. She's a fascist. She insults my wife in word and deed. And Ninochka's never laid a finger on anyone in all her young life . . ."

Nicky loved her, the simple, decent fellow, loved her madly. And that's how it all began . . .

Sergey Sergeyevich, sit still. Don't move. Do you see

135

a rat running around under the bed? Take a boot off without being noticed and hit it. Only be sure you don't miss. Otherwise it'll escape. There! Look, it'll pop its nose out again in a moment. So you throw your boot at its head. Kill it outright. Now!

Oh, you've missed! Hit it, Sergey! Bash it! Get it with the bottle! The bottle! . . .

What are you doing, you clumsy fellow? I told you to hit it with the bottle! Phew! Even my legs are trembling. My nerves are completely shattered.

But do you know who that was, Sergey Sergeyevich? Why, that was Ninochka come to visit us . . . She misses her dear Nicky. And that's why our Ninochka visits the old place . . .

(3)

Don't be frightened—I came in without knocking. My business is urgent. It's trouble, Sergey Sergeyevich, big trouble! That Krovatkina has nosed out the whole story and told Anchutker. What will happen to us now? What will happen?

Listen, I mustn't be found in your room. Especially in my natural form. The tenants might notice. As it is, I came in through a crack. Crawled under the door. At my age . . .

Just a minute! I'll just camouflage myself a little and then we'll talk.

What suitable objects have you got here? Aha! Let me

be a glass, and you sit down at the table as if you were drinking. If anyone comes in, just talk to yourself. Let them think you're a drunk. It's safer that way.

Right, come here—I'm already on the table. You see, you had three glasses and now you have four. No, no, not that one! How unobservant you are, really! Here I am, here! Near the plate.

Hey! Don't touch me! Next thing you'll be dropping me on the floor and breaking me. My legs ache enough already without that.

Sergey Sergeyevich, listen carefully and hear me out in all seriousness. Our position couldn't be worse. We have been discovered. An investigation is being made. Anchutker has stopped saying good morning to me since yesterday. I know they want to put me on trial for betraying their secrets. Tomorrow at midnight a Soviet will assemble in the kitchen. That wouldn't matter, but Shestopalov is dissatisfied with me. He's issued an order. "We trusted him," he says, "so now he's striking up another friendship where he shouldn't. And his new friend's a writer—copies down all his words on paper. There may be unpleasant consequences. We must punish this chatterbox as a warning to others. But we'll deal with the writer separately. Thank heavens he's an alcoholic and will soon start imagining real devils."

Do you understand what this means, Sergey Sergeyevich? They will separate us. They'll take away my last human being, deprive me of my home and roof. They'll send me under the floor. Into the damp and cold to join the micro-organisms. Or they'll launch me head first along the sewage system. And I'll be compelled to circulate there until the end of the world. Like the Eternal Jew called Ahasuerus. Have you read the novel of that name by Eugene Sue? Well, there you are. It'll be done the same way. From one toilet to another.

You're in for it too. They'll surround you with loathsome snouts, specters, and vampires. You'll be terrified. You'll take to drinking more than ever before. And the more you drink, the more terrified you'll be. Until you go off your rocker like poor Nikolay Nikolayevich!

You must escape. It's all been taken care of. I'll call for you tomorrow at half past eleven. Just before the festivities begin, before the Supreme Kitchen Soviet. Be ready. They'll be expecting guests and dressing up to the nines. They'll start preparing snacks. Made of carrion and rotten eggs. Very likely they'll lose their grip in the confusion. At that moment you put me in your pocket (and you can bet I'll do my best to squeeze in there somehow), put your overcoat on so I don't feel a draft, and go smartly out into the street. As if you'd had a bit to drink, and decided to take a stroll and get a breath of fresh air.

At the beginning we'll manage somehow in a hotel. And after that we'll set up house in an apartment. One without co-tenants and neighbors, where we're our own masters. "Without gods, tsars, or heroes," as the saying goes.

As a precaution against all eventualities you can hang up an ikon. Don't let that embarrass you—I'm used to it, having been brought up in the country. These superstitions are very common among country folk.

You say you don't want an ikon; your convictions don't

permit it? Then we'll manage with a simple reproduction. We'll cut out Raphael or someone with a baby out of *Universal History* and stick it up in a prominent place. It also gives good protection against the powers of darkness and the evil eye. And it's completely respectable and progressive. After all, it's art and no one can pick holes in that.

The great thing is to stick together, Sergey Sergeyevich. I'll never get away from here in all eternity without help from you, a human being. I can walk around inside the premises to my heart's content, on the walls and ceiling if I like. But I can't put a foot over the threshold. Physiological laws forbid it.

And you too (I speak without false modesty) will be lost without me. Whereas with me, God willing, you'll become world-famous. A Charles Dickens, a Mayne Reid. You see I know, I know all, you cunning fellow, you. When I come through the door, you take up your pen. Even when you're not quite yourself and have a poor command of the language . . .

But what do our conversations add up to? Just a miserable fragment. I've enough of these fairy tales to fill a whole *Decameron*. All based on personal experience. You can publish them in five volumes. With illustrations. We'll run rings around the Brothers Grimm, you and I, Sergey Sergeyevich.

Hey there! What on earth are you doing? Why are you pouring brandy into me? I'll choke, choke! Splash it out at once . . .

I must say, you gave me a fright, Sergey Sergeyevich.

Be sure there's none of this tomorrow! Not a single drop!
Be vigilant, careful, both in deed and word. Refrain, pray,
from brusque phrases containing allusions. You know
what happens otherwise. Did you see Ninochka yesterday? Yes, that's right, Ninochka in the form of a rat.
And now she'll stay that way—there's no going back.

Nicky put up with it for a long while, but once he burst
out, "Oh, the hell with you, Ninochka. I'm fed up with
these scandals."

And just as he pronounced these fatal words, Anchutker
came into the room. As if he'd come for a purpose, to get
a cigarette. And he stared intently at Ninochka, who
looked at Anchutker, and they took a great liking to each
other at that moment.

By that time Ninochka was no longer what she had
been. Her hair had grown thin, her eyes had sunk, while
her tummy had gone the opposite way and acquired a
bulge. And do you know, her behind had also become
notably bulky. In a word, she struck his fancy, and they
began to have meetings, pinchings, tender scratchings and
all that sort of thing. She turned into a complete witch.
Made her peace with Krovatkina, and even began to learn
the art of riding about at night on the lavatory pan. Like
a jet engine. Worked on intestinal gas.

But when they took Nikolay Nikolayevich off to the
lunatic asylum, her paramour abandoned her. Abandoned
her in a state of pregnancy. And to appease Avdotya's
jealousy and avoid paying alimony, they turned her into
a dumb animal in a corresponding condition. Then she
gave birth to little rats in a hole. Produced seven of them.

Perhaps you are sorry for her. But I see a genuine allegory in this incident. She undermined the foundations of morality, so it serves her right, and I even regret very much that you didn't hit her on the head with your boot. That would have been an excellent thing and a worthy revenge. For poor old Nicky. Like in *Anna Karenina*. He was a decent fellow.

I've got quite carried away chatting to you. Obviously Shestopalov was right when he called me a chatterbox. But that's easily said! I'm cut off from human habitation and there's no one to talk to. You don't speak, don't speak for days on end. And nights. Find yourself shuffling your felt slippers on the parquet floor.

Right, then, the important thing is to get out of here. The stories I know about Shestopalov—make you die laughing.

All right, it's decided! Until tomorrow then. You give me your word? All right then.

Now I'll retire the way I came, unnoticed. Don't be nervous, please. No one has seen us, no one has heard us. It's in the bag.

(4)

Hey!

Sergey Sergeyevich!

It's time.

The very hour!

Where are you? Where have you hidden yourself?

Has he gone away? Gone away without me! Abandoned an old fellow to be torn to pieces. A homeless old fellow . . .

What's that? What's that? Spread out on the floor? Surely he's not dead. Sergey Sergeyevich, my dear chap . . . His heart's beating. He's blinking. Wake up! Let's escape from here. The time is ripe. They've just called up —Shestopalov is expected at the festivities. Any moment now. They're not worried about us now . . . They're busy with preparations.

But what's the meaning of this, Sergey Sergeyevich? . . . And I thought— You ought to be ashamed of yourself! Gave your promise too . . . A fine time you've found . . . Couldn't control yourself . . .

But how can you walk on the street in a state like that? You'll be run in.

Anyway, get up! We have four minutes' grace. Stand up, I tell you!

What do you mean, you *can't?* That you've lost the use of your legs? Stop playing the fool!

Come on, old pal, let's try it together. Make an effort. Put your arms around my neck. Right! Try again. I must say you're no featherweight, chum. Stop, stop, don't fall over!

Sh-sh-sh! Have you gone out of your mind! Clattering through the apartment like that. If they suspect, they'll come for us. And where shall I hide? I'm asking you, aren't I—what am I supposed to do?

Well, what is it you're muttering? The hell with your apologies. Do you hear, do you hear? Krovatkina's put-

ting her ear to the door. We're sunk. Now she'll call Anchutker, Shestopalov . . .

Sergey Sergeyevich! Get me out of this, son! At least
get on your knees. Let me help you. There you are.
There. Now pray. I'll hold on from behind by your shoulders. Pray! Say your prayers, I tell you, you drunken
bastard!

What do you mean, you've forgotten them? How am I
supposed to know? It's you who have to know. It's you
who's human, not me. This is right up your alley. I'm
not allowed to; it's not done.

What's the meaning of this, Sergey Sergeyevich—you
live among devils, write stories about devils, and haven't
learned to pray!

All right, we'll do it lying down. Turn on your back.
Will you get it into your head that this is our only hope?
As if I'd have asked you otherwise! Put your fingers together. The forehead first. Now over here . . . Why are
you pretending? You're putting it on. Snore or not, as you
like, I won't believe you. You're fully conscious and understand everything . . . Oh, really, are you the devil
himself or what?

And who's this? Ah-h! Ninochka, is it? Hello, Ninochka . . . Don't be afraid, don't be afraid. I won't
touch you. It's all the same to me now . . .

There! Just admire this handsome fellow. Your future
husband. The third in the series. You'll settle down together in a rat hole . . . Smell his eyes, smell them.
Lick him. He'll let you . . . He's not interested in you
at the moment. He feels sick and the room's going around.

143

And little devils are already jumping about before his eyes. Rats too.

Well, this is it. The whole gang of them is trooping along, stamping along the corridor. Now they'll break in. It's me they've come for. And for you too, Sergey Sergeyevich. You too. You too.

1959

AT THE CIRCUS

THE MUSIC crashed out again. A dazzling light flashed on and two acrobats, sisters who were as strong as bears, performed an act called "the acrobatic dance." They rode on each other in a standing position and upside down, driving their red heels into each other's brawny shoulders, and executed exotic sequences of every possible kind with arms as thick as legs and legs as thick as torsos. Their bodies, prodigiously splayed, were steaming.

Then a whole family of jugglers, consisting of a man and wife with four children, leaped into the ring. They did uncanny gyrations in the air, while Dad, who was the chief juggler and had trained them, squinted his eyes at

147

the bridge of his nose and stuck in his mouth a stick with a nickel-plated disk, placing on it a bottle labeled "Zhigulyovskoye Beer," and on the bottle a glass, and on top of that—first an umbrella, then a dish, and finally two decanters containing real water on top of the dish. For what must have been more than half a minute he held all this in his teeth and didn't spill anything.

But all were outshone by a performer called the Manipulator, a sort of genteel little intellectual of foreign appearance. He had jet-black hair with a part as smooth as if he'd had the bare patch cut out by an electric razor run along a ruler. Below it he had a mustache and the complete outfit—a natty little tie, patent-leather shoes.

He went up with an innocent air to a lady and extracted a live white mouse from her hat; then a second, a third, and so on, until there were nine of them. The lady looked as if she was about to faint. "Oh, dear," she said, "I can't stand any more of it," and asked for water to calm her nerves.

He next ran up to her escort on the right side and seized him carefully by the nose, with two fingers, like a barber. With his unoccupied left hand he took a wineglass out of his pocket and held it up to the light so that everyone could see that it was really empty. Then, with an abrupt move, he pinched the man's nose, and out poured a fizzy, golden soft drink into the wineglass. Without spilling a drop, he offered it politely to the lady, who drank it with pleasure and said, *"Merci,"* while everyone around laughed and clapped their hands in delight.

148

As soon as the audience was silent the Manipulator turned to the ring and in a rude voice asked the man from whom he had just drawn the soft drink, "Tell me quickly, my man, what's the time by your watch?"

The man put a hand to his vest, but there was nothing there, and the Manipulator, tensing himself slightly, spat out his gold watch onto the ring. Then he returned other people's things in the same way—one got back a wallet, another a cigarette case, and a third some unconsidered trifle like a penknife or a comb—all the things he'd managed to extract during his performance. He even pinched an old man's bank book and an article for private feminine use out of a secret pocket. And he returned everything to its destination amid general applause, so great an artist was he!

When it was all over and the audience had begun to disperse, Konstantin felt fed up with his own lack of skill—he could neither turn cartwheels in orbit nor ride a bicycle like a crab, with his hands on the pedals and his feet holding the handlebars and steering in different directions. Without previous practice he probably couldn't even throw his cap in the air so as to make it perform a somersault and land smartly on his skull. The only thing Konstantin could do was to stick a Russian cigarette in his mouth back to front without burning himself and quietly puff smoke out of the mouthpiece as if from the funnel of a locomotive or steamer.

But nowadays every schoolboy knew this simple trick, and Konstantin was twenty-five and fed up with everything—having to climb up and down walls for days on end like a lunatic and unscrew blown fuses with no other pleasures in life except movies and girls.

He got up and made for the exit with that determined springy gait employed by no one in the world except conjurers and acrobats.

An opportunity presented itself straightway, in the shape of a man, a hell of a fellow in a fur-lined coat unbuttoned over its whole façade, who was blocking the central doorway with his broad figure and saying to someone—it wasn't clear who—"Real women acrobats ought to be seen without any clothes on. And not in a circus, but in an apartment, on a tablecloth, in the middle of pineapples . . ."

His eyes, which were blue with green flecks, were focused on something distant and he paid not the slightest attention to Konstantin. And Konstantin suddenly barged in and got stuck in the most crucial position, face to face with the man in the doorway, in the thick of the crush. They jostled each other, and ended up by getting so mixed up that it was hard to tell which was which. The fur coat flung its fluffy interior even wider apart, while the broad-chested, double-breasted jacket opened up by itself, and all this occurred like magic, without human intervention . . .

I catch my breath and my pulse moves into my fingers. They tick in time with the encircled heart which beats in the other man's breast—near the inner pocket, and it jumps out neatly onto my palm without suspecting the switch or having an inkling of my exciting, otherworldly

presence. And now with a single sweep of the hand I perform a miracle—a fat wad of money flies through the
air like a bird and settles under my shirt. "Your money's
fine and now it's mine," as the song has it, and it is this
fabulous conversion that constitutes the entire trick.

The money is warm from the warmth of your body,
dear comrade, and has a tender, perfumed smell like a
girl's neck. And you are still proud of this money, though
possessing nothing, and puff out your empty chest as you
talk about women acrobats, laughing in anticipation, but
laughing and anticipating in vain. Because it is I who
shall take a taxi to the Kiev Restaurant in your place, eat
your sardines, drink all the cognac, and kiss your women
instead of you—at your personal expense, but to my full
satisfaction. I don't intend to be stingy, and if we meet in
the restaurant I'll stand you drinks enough to make you
tipsy and feed you till you can hardly stand—with that
very food you yourself did not manage to consume in
time. What's more, you'll be grateful to me for this, I
make so bold as to assure you. You'll think that I'm some
writer, performer, or sports celebrity. But all I am is a
conjurer-manipulator. Let's get acquainted. Greetings!

In the dark of the street Konstantin pulled up his
collar, and it was only then that he managed to set his
facial muscles in motion. They scarcely obeyed him, and
seemed to be made of India rubber, so that if you hit them
with your fist it would bounce off. But Konstantin manipu-
lated his mouth in the direction of his ears and back until
he had restored the original suppleness to his whole face.
Then he lit a cigarette, stuck the lighted end in his mouth,

and set off, puffing smoke out of the stem, to the nearest taxi stand.

Since then a new life has begun for Konstantin Petrovich. He looks in at the Kiev Restaurant from time to time, and hardly has he crossed the threshold before brilliantined waiters rush from the inner depths, exclaiming in staccato voices like gunshots, "Coming, coming, coming, sir!"

Each one has above his head a tray that constantly revolves, and on it are different wines—red and white, or there's one called "Pink Muscatelle." In other words, the whole gamut is at your service, Konstantin Petrovich.

"No," says Konstantin Petrovich in a tired voice, politely removing them with his hand. "I'm definitely abstaining. I don't feel well and I don't want anything at all. But give me some common or garden variety—nine and a half ounces of it—and a tiny piece of bread and Atlantic herring. Only don't use black bread to go with the sardine, but give me white currant bread, the kind with juicy currants."

And at once the waiters, three in number, uncork colored bottles and flick napkins in the air, polishing goblets and wineglasses until they shine like mirrors and whisking specks of dust off their narrow-pointed boots in mid-flight.

When you've drunk nine and a half ounces for form's sake, all your senses become extremely acute. You distinguish clearly both the grind of sliding knives, which sets your teeth on edge and causes convulsions of the spinal cord, and the bell-like ringing of glass put to the lips on different levels, and the monotonous refrain of men's voices: "Your health! To your arrival! To our next meeting! To your arrival!"—and the quizzical laughter of women who are waiting for something while constantly turning their heads around and nervously titivating themselves as if they were going to a wedding.

An apelike dexterity may be discerned in the posturings of the waiters. They jump between the tubs and the palms that grow everywhere, as in Africa, and toss sets of tin plates full of steaming borshch to and fro, or, bent over your table as if they were playing billiards, pour out, with a brief downward movement, everything you want into glasses.

When the full picture of the half-tipsy restaurant suddenly revealed itself distinctly to Konstantin Petrovich's gaze, he felt in the depths of his soul (somewhere in the core of the spine) a sweet, piercing quiver that set his hair in motion. As if he was walking along a wire a hundred feet high, and, though the walls were tottering and threatening to collapse, he walked on with a light, measured, elastic stride, perfectly evenly, in a straight line. The audience was watching intently, holding its breath and placing its hope in you as in God: "Konstantin, don't betray us! Konstantin Petrovich, don't let us down! Show them what's what!"

And you must, absolutely *must* put something on for them—some kind of *salto mortale* or other stupendous trick—or else hit on and utter some quite extraordinary word, after which the whole world will turn upside down and pass into a supernatural condition in the twinkling of an eye. The heart beats about in your breast like a bird in a cage; your soul is rent in fragments by love and pity, while you keep pouring out more and more vodka to continue the torment, until finally you rise up to your full height from the befouled parquet floor and bark out a series of unprintable obscenities so that all Europe can hear you . . .

After this Konstantin Petrovich had the habit of calming down. Now tranquil, he would invite anyone who wished to come to his table for free hospitality and a heart-to-heart talk. The one who joined him most frequently of all was a certain sad man, elderly and modestly dressed, who, incidentally, was Jewish, though an alcoholic, and maintained on his emaciated chest a decorous dark blue bow tie as a sign that he had received a higher education. His name was Solomon, and he would ensconce himself in a dark corner under a palm tree, patiently waiting for a vacancy, for he disposed of no funds and they let him sit in the restaurant mainly because of his cultured appearance.

"Now then, Solomon Moiseyevich, since you're an educated man, while I didn't even get through the tenth grade properly, tell me without delay—what is the essence of things? And be sure you get this same essence in a single word . . ."

Solomon would wrinkle his brows, trying to recollect all the branches of learning which he had studied in various institutes of learning. "Essence of a phenomenon . . .

phenomena . . . idea . . ." he would say falteringly, without being able to remember a single thing more.

Then Konstantin Petrovich would offer him a glass to dispose him to conversation, but not more than two ounces, otherwise Solomon Moiseyevich would lose his human aspect and be incapable of keeping him company in intimate conversation.

"All right then, all right, you've had your drink and you can be patient for a bit! Talk to me as one human being to another. Answer me—why am I a rogue and a drunkard, and why am I lost to shame? Come on, tell me, why are Russians always trying to steal something? Stealing or drinking. What's the origin of this spiritual need in the Russian?"

Solomon Moiseyevich knew the scientific answer to this, and, shyly nibbling on a pickle, would go back in his search for the causal origin as far as the Tartar Yoke, which was what started the tavern and the prison on Russian soil—the whole thing due to cultural backwardness.

"Now in England, Konstantin Petrovich, you'd be an inventor . . . or a Member of Parliament . . . a minister without portfolio . . ."

His disproportionately large Adam's apple darted up and down his emaciated throat, and his eyes cast anguished, foreign glances at the ceiling. But just the same he couldn't pierce into the very root of life. Anyway, how could a Solomon Moiseyevich understand the soul of a Russian? And though he was an alcoholic for personal reasons deriving from his race, who was he to offer

England or Belgium or some sort of freedom of the press in exchange? That was also far from clear.

"I'll go and rob your British treasury! And I'll drink the proceeds, gamble 'em away till I haven't got a stitch to stand up in! But what about my soul? Why has it been given to me? I ask you about the soul, you brood of Judas, and instead of the soul you give me this crap!"

But Konstantin Petrovich never hit him—on the contrary, he would give him an extra drink, a second and a third one, and all because Solomon possessed conversational gifts. Another person may get drunk on your money and you find him angling to recount his life story in sequence—to you, who stood him the drinks! You can't get a word in edgewise. But this fellow does a little arguing or falls into a reverie as the need arises—or just sits and preserves a sympathetic silence.

Sometimes Konstantin Petrovich would become upset and the tears would flow, and he'd weep and sob so that nothing could comfort him. And he'd keep talking about his unhappy life and remembering his old mother, who, only three yards away from this very spot, was lying on an iron bedstead and dying of hunger, while he, the bastard, instead of running to her and immediately taking her the means to cure herself, was hanging around here drinking away every penny he possessed with the scum of the earth.

Solomon Moiseyevich would go on listening and just sigh and say nothing. And though he knew for a certainty that Konstantin Petrovich didn't have any mother and that the whole story was a mere fantasy concocted to intensify his grief, he never tried to disillusion him because, well, he was a human being himself and understood that everyone has the urge to call himself a bastard. And when Konstantin Petrovich started hiccupping as a result of his sad experiences and banging his head on the table and on the chair and on whatever came to hand, he only took him gently by the shoulder and said, "Don't carry on like that, Konstantin. Let's have a drink instead. And let's move on quickly to less gloomy topics. For example, it's been a long time since we talked about God. What's your opinion —does God exist?"

At this joke of Solomon's, Konstantin would stop crying and gradually begin laughing, understanding the delicate allusion to the fact that there are no gods or devils in this world, though it would be very amusing if there were.

He'd had occasion to peep into churches. And he loved all those miracles depicted on ceilings and walls in acrobatic postures. He was especially pleased by one joker who got himself up as a dead man and then jumped out of his grave and astonished everyone. And another fellow, who, incidentally, belonged to the same nation as Solomon Moiseyevich, treacherously informed against him, but they didn't catch the joker, they caught the traitor Judas instead and nailed him alive to the church cross . . .

Listening to these stories, Solomon Moiseyevich rejoiced and kept repeating delightedly that the church originated in the circus, and that nothing was more important to the Russian people than tricks and miracles.

But what Konstantin Petrovich liked more than churches was to go to the Sandunovsky Baths—to the family cubicles. Here they admitted only married people, asking for their identity cards as proof, but by a happy coincidence Konstantin had a friend on the staff who'd been disabled in the war, a chap called Lyoshka, and Lyoshka fixed things so that a fellow could even share a bath with a general's wife as long as he didn't start a fight.

Thanks to this acquaintance, Konstantin bathed on a bachelor basis with a girl called Tamara, and they got up to such acrobatics in these cubicles as can neither be fabled in story nor portrayed by pen. No matter who you told about it, no one would believe it, though it was enough to make anyone envious.

"Should we have some sport, eh?" he'd ask Tamara, latching the door.

"We'll have some sport," Tamara would say in a normal voice, but with a tremendous wriggle of her backside.

And, throwing off their clothes, down to the last undergarment, they would begin to demonstrate various unusual tricks. Konstantin Petrovich would hang a pail between his legs in an intriguing fashion and beat a tattoo on it like a drum, while Tamara danced folk dances. Crimson, breathless, and covered with silver foam, she cantered around the bath, which was as hot as Africa, while he ran after her with a clatter of iron, and they looked like devils in the steam of hell itself, and also like Indian redskins, who really do exist and go about naked and shameless.

When Tamara got tired of showing off to no purpose, Konstantin Petrovich would invent other diversions. He'd pour cold water over her. Or he'd feed her with soap instead of a kiss, or else, at the other end, to keep the party going and introduce the element of surprise, he'd use his index finger or shove in an indelible pencil.

Loving Tamara permitted him everything. She banned only one thing: laughing out of place when the players were entering ecstasy and beginning to function in unison with terrifying strength.

At these times Konstantin Petrovich was seized with laughter. But Tamara, biting her lip, threatened him with her pink eyes. Her face, hot and dark, seemed embittered. "Be quiet!" she would whisper. "Silence! Don't you dare laugh!"

Then she'd collapse on one side and become docile again, being the first to laugh at what had happened. Before the event and after it you could laugh to your heart's content, but during it—no.

"It's a sin, a grave sin!" she would assert with conviction, but she was unable to explain her fancies.

"Yes, yes! That's the way it is!" Solomon Moiseyevich would shout, growing progressively more intoxicated as the narrative proceeded. By the time the story of Konstantin Petrovich's amorous frolics was finished, he would be properly drunk. "A sin! Thou shalt not sin!" he'd shout in his excitement. "Play on, the sky's the limit! Thou shalt not kill! Thou shalt not kill! God! Devil! *Ridi, Pagliaccio, in su tu amor infranto* . . ."

As if he'd been let off a leash he would start talking a lot of nonsense about the enigmatic Russian character, pulling at his gigantic Adam's apple, and about the enigmatic nature of women—all this in a terrible state of excitement. Everyone knew that three years before, Solomon's wife, a lascivious Russian bitch, had run away, after first robbing him and then disgracing him with the hairdresser Gennady, aged sixteen. He knew women and feared them, having every reason to do so. But what could he understand about the Russian national character, this Solomon Moiseyevich?

Lyoshka, the disabled soldier, knew a valuable saying: "A sapper makes only one mistake." Lyoshka himself had practical experience of the aptness of this piece of folk wisdom—a fascist mine had blown off his right arm at Berlin.

But the commission of this error and his irreparable loss had not taught him any sense, and so one-armed Lyoshka once said to Konstantin, "Do you know, Konstantin, or don't you, that I have my eye on a private apartment with three rooms and a balcony and all? The landlord had to go to Tallin the day before yesterday in connection with his work, and his wife is staying in their country cottage with their son Vovochka, who's suffered from rickets since birth, and needs to get a breath of fresh air regularly. And Vovochka's governess, who was supposed to protect their property, was no sooner left alone than she started playing around until daybreak with the guys from the trolley depot, and is there any reason why she shouldn't put in a night shift there today? What's your opinion?"

"I fully understand the nature of your foreign policy," says Konstantin, "only you're handling me in a very vul-

gar fashion. I deal with living beings, and it is not my
habit to climb into closed windows heaven knows how
many floors up from the ground. Anyway, is this apartment of yours with the balcony a worthwhile job? It would
be a better idea if you'd bring me some Zhigulyovskoye
beer into the cubicle."

"Come off it, Konstantin, and stop building yourself
up as a great *artiste*," Lyoshka tells him in an irritated
voice. "And don't paw Tamara with two hands at the same
time in my presence. It's almost indecent. Put your pants
on and let's think about it. A sapper makes only one mistake."

So they talked until late at night, and when the Sandunovsky baths closed they took Solomon Moiseyevich
along as look-out man, along with a Browning revolver
(just in case of trouble) which Lyoshka had removed
from the field of battle during the war, and set off without
delay to the place where that little apartment that had
everything was waiting.

It was on the first floor, a three-room apartment packed
to the ceiling with expensive junk: gabardine and wools,
two natty suits of foreign make and a chocolate-colored
leather overcoat called a "raglan"—stood and laughed
at them. All the doors, windows, and even the small
transoms were bolted with double locks, and there wasn't
a single little hole, or even crack, to be found. A natural
question arose: how to get in.

You are of course astonished at this hopeless prospect,
and are tearing your hair, prepared in your imbecility
to adopt the trite procedure of going through the window

with unbelievable noise and clatter. But that's not it, you haven't got the point, and you won't solve this problem in a lifetime.

But there exists in the world, just between ourselves, a certain instrument, called, in plain language, a "skeleton key." With that no door holds terrors. As for padlocks, they can be dealt with by a collection of keys adapted for every vicissitude of life.

It was so quiet on all sides, fellows, that it made you want to cry.

"Pull the blinds or we'll be seen from outside," Konstantin ordered one-armed Lyoshka and fingered the revolver. "I'll take the raglan, and the cane too."

He'd taken a liking to the knob of the cane, which was split in two halves like a pair of buttocks, but on a smaller scale. You walk along the pavement with the cane and keep feeling the knob, and you can show it to girls to amuse and embarrass them when you first meet them. A thing like that you've simply got to have available both at home and when you go for a walk.

Suddenly Konstantin senses that someone is unexpectedly asleep in the next room. In he goes and sees in the bed—whom would you guess? The lady of the house? No! Her husband? Wrong again! A sleeping governess with only a nightgown on? That would have been all right, but just the same, you're wrong. Wrong again! Made another boner! What he sees is a little guy not unknown to you, with pleasant little whiskers, but without his tie and without his hair parting. Actually the hair parting, in the form of a piece of cloth, is hanging separately on the back of a chair, and next to it stand the patent-leather shoes in parade order, but otherwise there isn't a single other soul here.

An absolutely genuine Manipulator from a genuine circus was emitting full-throated snores from the householder's bed, or pretending to snore while getting ready to spring.

As turned out subsequently, the Manipulator—bad luck to his bald pate—had trotted off that night to see his childhood friend and get some rest from his family, but instead of that had got involved in Konstantin's nocturnal manipulations—to their mutual displeasure and with a tragic denouement.

But Konstantin knew nothing of this at that climactic moment, and he was very disillusioned by the sudden appearance of a guest whose magical agility was known to him from his regular Sunday visits to the state circus. This devilish prestidigitator could strip anyone of his possessions with his bare hands and steal anything you like, so Konstantin directed his firearm at his mentor in case he should awaken and decide to get up to one of his tricks.

"Don't make so much noise messing around in the chest of drawers," he commanded Lyoshka in a whisper. "And don't forget—I'm taking the cane with the knob like a backside."

Whether it was because of these words or something else, the Manipulator opened his eyes till they nearly bulged out of his head, and Konstantin did not have time to warn him, "Be quiet, or I'll fire," before he shouted

163

at the top of his voice, which had a repulsive ring, "Help! Murder!"

In the majority of cases men who face a leveled revolver put their hands up and say nothing, looking as if they'd been bewitched. But women, contrary to all reason, screech and thrash around and occasionally bite, though it's possible to make them see the situation from the other fellow's point of view so that they cry into a cushion in the interests of survival.

But this time Konstantin had come up against a real villain who paid no attention to the barrel of the Browning. With his eyes bulging out onto his cheeks, he climbed out of the bed onto the floor, and, just as he was, in a condition of utter daze and in an unprepossessing state of nature, lunged at the balcony door. The glass crashed into smithereens and over the whole street, above the peaceful roofs, bombinated the multiple echo: "Help! Help! Murder!"

Then, to cut short an ugly scandal that was getting on his nerves, Konstantin, almost in tears, fired at his back between the anemic shoulder blades, wherein lay his, Konstantin's, fatal error—and, as you know, comrades, a sapper makes only one mistake. Because if you think the thing out correctly, what was needed was not to shoot and let off dangerous noises, but to let the Manipulator have it on his bare temple with some blunt instrument— for example, the revolver butt—and to continue the inspection of the premises without unnecessary noise after silencing the rowdy fellow.

But Konstantin, instead of acting decisively, had lightly

pressed the release spring with a finger, and that malicious German spring had done its job automatically—
and that's all there was to it. That's all there was to it;
but the Manipulator had grown silent at once. He wasn't
shouting any more, but his lips were bubbling, and he was
whining and gurgling in his throat, producing with extreme care long and rather hoarse trills in the complicated art of gargling in the upper and lower registers.

It seemed at first that, after a spell of such antics done
for the sake of effect, he'd sit down on the floor, finish the
coughing-up process, and announce for all to hear that
he had taken them in so as to frighten them. But clearly
this was an *artiste* giving a performance fit for outside
consumption, who, inspired by Konstantin's shot, was
playing his star role, transforming himself miraculously
into a dead man conscious of his superiority over those
who had remained alive. His face retreated as smoothly as
a sailing boat, acquiring the innate pride of stone and petrified water. He died unobtrusively without so much as a
farewell wink, and left Konstantin in bewilderment at the
trick which had been performed, and which belonged to
them both in equal measure.

This spectacle was spoiled by the appearance of Solomon Moiseyevich. He had honorably stood watch in the
dark, damp entrance, and he now ran into the room,
gasping from high blood pressure, to inform his friends of
the catastrophe that threatened them from awakened doorkeepers and unsleeping policemen.

"Why did you make a noise, Konstantin Petrovich?"
he asked with deep anguish, noticing nothing of his sur-

roundings. "After all, I did warn you to be careful. A pistol can fire without any pressure on the trigger—from the ordinary movement of the air . . ."

Konstantin wasn't arguing the point . . . In the doorway two hefty janitors were twisting Lyoshka's only arm, the left one, behind his back. Lyoshka was trying to fight them off with his legs and saying, "Let me go, you bastards!"

Realizing that resistance was useless, Konstantin put his hands up, but still couldn't deny himself a small pleasure—he fired off all the rounds remaining in the Browning at the ceiling, thereby leaving a merry, goodhearted memento of himself. The policemen fell to the floor, then hurled themselves at Konstantin and pretty quickly disarmed him. Thus in the flower of beauty and health was destroyed the young life of Konstantin Petrovich.

True, before the dismal finale he did have a good performance before a great gathering of the public in court. He happened to get a strict public prosecutor of the right kind, who demanded the extreme penalty by shooting for Konstantin Petrovich. And the defense counsel, who was also no fool, kept insisting on the extenuating feeblemindedness of the accused. The eyes of all men and women were riveted on Konstantin Petrovich, and, as he stood in the center of the ring, he experienced many wonderful moments that tickled his jealous artistic vanity.

The court sentenced Konstantin Petrovich to twenty years' imprisonment with confiscation of property, both real estate and chattels. But he'd lost the raglan and his

revered cane long before, and now, having dodged the
firing squad, wasn't too bothered by the period that lay
ahead.

Lyoshka and Solomon Moiseyevich got ten years
apiece.

One fine morning Konstantin was walking unhurriedly
to work in a column of people who, like himself, had been
roughly used by fate. They kept their hands folded behind their backs as a sign of their lost freedom and oblig-
atory submissiveness. Around them were darting birds,
the free denizens of the region, and there was a heady
smell of flowers, grass, and bushes. Transparent, light
dandelion heads were flying around everywhere. On either
side, reeling from boredom and their own insignificance, a
small posse of guards drifted along, smoking large home-
made cigarettes.

Suddenly against the background of this peaceful landscape a disturbance occurred. An old jailer threw down
his half-smoked cigarette and emitted a terrified howl.
"Stop! Stop or I fire!"

But Konstantin was already hurtling over hillocks and
humps, pushing off from the soft earth with his sinewy
legs. The wind played serenely about his animated face.
Far away could be seen the mauve forest—eternal refuge
of legendary highwaymen.

Konstantin beheld an expanse suffused with electric
light and miles of wire extended beneath the vault of a
worldwide circus. And the farther he flew away from the
initial point of his escape, the more joyous and alarmed

did his spirits become. He was gripped by a feeling akin to inspiration, which made every vein leap and cavort, and, in its cavorting, await the onflow of that extraneous and magnanimous supernatural power that hurls one into the air in a mighty leap, the highest and easiest in your lightweight life.

Ever nearer and nearer . . . Now it would hurl him up . . . now he would show them . . .

Konstantin leaped, turned over, and, performing the long-awaited somersault, fell, shot through the head, face downward on the ground.

1955

GRAPHOMANIACS

(A Story from My Life)

❀❀❀❀❀❀❀

I MET the poet Galkin on my way ιo the publishing office. We exchanged restrained bows, and I was thinking of moving on when he suddenly came up to me, suggesting that we should eat an ice cream and drink a bottle of cranberry cordial at his expense.

It was hot and stuffy. Pushkin Boulevard was sweltering, and the breath of an approaching thunderstorm could be sensed in the air. The phrase appealed to me. I must memorize it and use it: "the breath of an approaching thunderstorm could be sensed in the air." With this phrase I would end my novel *In Search of Joy*. I would make a point of inserting it, if necessary in proof. An approaching storm would enliven the landscape and

171

harmonize with the novel's events, introducing a faint hint of revolution and of the love of my hero Vadim for Tatyana Krechet.

I knew that Galkin had a foible—a readiness to recite his works to all and sundry, even including bus conductors. And so it turned out. While I was refreshing myself with the ice cream and drinking the sharp-flavored cordial, he contrived to unload upon me nearly two dozen verse lines. They included "hairy legs," "pilasters," and "chrysanthemums." I don't remember any more—it was the usual rubbish.

I dislike verse. It is bad for the mind, turning it in an unnecessary direction. You start thinking in rhyme and speaking in rhyme, which has a terribly harmful effect —especially on the creation of prose. I was doing my best not to listen to Galkin, and in order to distract myself from the poetry I began to look him over; for observation of a person's exterior may almost always prove useful.

It was a typical specimen of failure which was rocking itself on the chair in front of me. An unshaven neck protruded from a grubby collar, while a certain sheepish quality was imparted by the thick lips and flattened nose. He was reciting affectedly, drawling out the words as if singing, and rolling up the whites of his eyes in ecstasy. He had fallen into a condition of trance. His face had stopped sweating and become pinched, taking on a silver-ish, metallic glint.

I was afraid of our attracting attention in the café and gave a warning cough, but Galkin noticed nothing and went on with his declamation. Suddenly in the middle of a line he stumbled and leaned straight forward, shuffling his empty lips in search of a word which had escaped his memory as a drowning man gasps for breath before going to the bottom. Instead of the continuation a groan, full of pain and passion, broke from him: "M-m-m-oo-oo!" Unable to put the brake on his voice, he gave vent to this devastating bellow: "M-m-m-oo-oo!"

That was the end of the performance, and only a second later Galkin was speaking with contrived nonchalance. "How do you like it, friend? How do you like my compulsive scribbling?"

He smiled skeptically. But what I noticed was that his thorax was quaking, while his temples pulsated violently as fresh drops of sweat, the signs of exhaustion, appeared on them.

I gave a laugh, and after laughing gently as long as was necessary, said, "Very strange, Semyon," said I. "Very, very strange. Do you really mean to say that your works"—I deliberately said "works"—"seem to you to be compulsive scribbling—graphomania, in other words?"

"Yes, I do. I do think so, damn it."

"And do you agree that everyone without exception should call you a graphomaniac? To your face? 'Graphomaniac Galkin! How do you do, Graphomaniac Semyon Galkin!' Nothing will make me believe that."

"Well, you're wrong!" he clamored, pleased at something. In his joy he took off from his chair and did an excited little dance. "Wrong, wrong! Because there's no

173

difference. Yes, yes, don't argue, I know best. Graphomania—it's a disease, the psychiatrists tell us, an in-
curable vicious urge to produce verses, plays, and novels
in defiance of the world. What talent, what genius, tell
me for heaven's sake—what genius has there been who
did not suffer from this noble malady? Any graphomaniac, believe you me, down to the lousiest and pettiest
of the tribe, in the depths of his feeble heart believes in
his own genius. And who knows, who can tell in advance?
After all, Shakespeare and Pushkin, say, were also graphomaniacs, graphomaniacs of genius . . . It's just that they
had luck. But if they hadn't had any luck, if they hadn't
been printed, what then?"

I followed Galkin's twists and turns with unaccountable
emotion. There was something about them which alter-
nately attracted and repelled me. I didn't know whether
it was his usual tomfoolery or whether he was arguing
seriously.

But Galkin had already lost heart. He had installed
himself at the table and seized his ice cream, which by
this time had melted and started to run. He scraped and
licked out his soggy cardboard cup, remarking while thus
engaged: "Mimicry, Paul Ivanovich. It's a means of
self-protection. I'm not trying to intrude on the ranks of
genius. But I am fed up—fed up, do you understand?
All you hear everywhere is 'graphomania, graphomania.'
A mediocrity, in other words. But I tell them (not aloud
of course, but privately, in the secret parts of my soul):
'To hell with the lot of you! After all, there are such people as drunkards, for example, there are profligates,

sadists, drug addicts . . . And I—I'm a graphomaniac! Like Pushkin, like Leo Tolstoy! And you leave me
alone!' Would you like me to recite something romantic,
friend? Out of my second book of verse? You do know
my second book?"

I knew perfectly well that during the whole of his life
Galkin had never published a single book, either a first
one or a second. True, there had been one or two translations and one little poem in a provincial newspaper to
mark an anniversary, but that was all. And I knew Galkin's habit of imagining himself a real writer with his
own line of development and chronology. His second
book, his fifth book—all in periods. The vainglorious
bombast of a graphomaniac.

I didn't want to put him in his place at the moment—
he looked too unhappy. I was ready to endure more of
his doggerel out of compassion, but I was in a hurry to
get to the publisher's and answered gently, "Let's have
you recite it some other time, Semyon. As it is I have to
go soon—they're expecting me at the publisher's."

And I told him briefly, without making any parade, of
the condition of my affairs, which at that time were very
promising. But my news produced no impression on Galkin, or else perhaps envy made him pretend to be unim-
pressed.

"Ah!" he said, yawning and stretching himself in
unseemly fashion. "They've been feeding you on promises
for twenty years. For twenty years they've been saying
they'd print you, but not one book have they brought out."

And once again he was off on his hobby horse. "We

live in a remarkable country. Everybody writes, including schoolgirls and old-age pensioners. I got to know a fellow here—Christ, what an ugly puss! And what a pair of fists! 'My dear comrade,' I tell him, 'you ought to take up boxing. You'd make a pile of money. You'd have fame too —and the admiration of the girls.' But he had his own line. 'No,' he says. 'I have another vocation,' he says. 'I was born for poetry.' 'Born,' if you understand me. Everyone has been 'born'! There's a universal popular leaning toward *belles lettres*. But do you know what we owe it to? To censorship. Yes, censorship is the dear old mother who's cherished us all. Abroad, things are simpler and harsher. Some lord brings out a wretched book of *vers libre*, and immediately it's spotted as crap. No one reads it and no one buys it, so the lord takes up useful work like energetics or stomatology . . . But we live our whole lives in pleasant ignorance, flattering ourselves with hopes . . . And this is marvelous! Why, damn it, the state itself gives you the right—the invaluable right—to regard yourself as an unacknowledged genius. And all your life, all your life you can—"

I got up.

"Wait! Wait!" he shouted. "One second! Here you and I have been talking to each other and looking at each other, but all the time we've been continuously thinking the same thing to ourselves. Each has been thinking, 'You are a graphomaniac, but I am a genius. I am a genius, but you are a graphomaniac.' "

"I must ask you not to call me a graphomaniac," I re-

176

plied curtly. "You can consider yourself what you like, but leave me out of it!"

"But of course, of course . . ."

His shoulders were shaking with silent hysterical laughter.

We parted coldly without shaking hands, just as we had met.

The young secretary raised a neat eyebrow. "Straustin? Paul Ivanovich?" She repeated her question as if she had heard my name for the first time and plunged into the desk drawer.

The door into the editor's office, upholstered in leatherette, was slightly open. Through it could be heard, accompanied by the typists' despondent rattle, the editor's castrated tenor, which I knew well.

". . . from the point of view of composition. From the point of view of language you're even weaker. 'The sun sweated in the clouds.' Do such things really happen? Can the sun really sweat? And in the clouds, at that? Study Chekhov. From the point of view of plot, why does your Nastya marry Ptitsyn? And why was that lieutenant (you know who)—what was his name—killed? . . ."

A second voice could be heard muttering and diffidently contradicting the speaker: "Second Lieutenant Greben. At Vyazma. That's what actually happened. Absolutely true. Died of a shot in the stomach. Altered his name a little. Name of Shpilkin. And there was a Nastya too. There was a Nastya. Called Zinka. Been gathering experience. For sixty-eight years. Retired colonel. Three wars, four wounds, two head concussions. Lots of material. Can't let it go to waste. Be of use in my free time. Composition can be changed. Can alter language. Perfectly correct, what you said. Don't mind throwing out the sun."

Being pretty much at home in the publishing business, I winked at the secretary. "Who's that, Zinochka? The latest graphomaniac? Poor Sevastyan Sevastyanych! So literature's being stormed by retired colonels of cavalry . . ."

But she didn't so much as move an eyebrow. Disdaining all sympathy, she didn't even so much as smile at my friendly jocularity. She closed the leatherette-upholstered door and, shoving some papers in the desk, answered in an official tone that my novel *In Search of Joy* wasn't in their records any longer. Allegedly it had been turned down by the publishers and dispatched to me at my home a week previously with a critical comment. There was a signature to the effect in the delivery column of the office messenger's book.

"There, you see? Do you recognize the signature? Is it your surname?"

I had recognized the handwriting, recognized too the bitterness of deceit and the black serpent of treachery inscribed in the delivery column in green ink. "Z. Straustin." Zinaida! My wife! But at the moment I wasn't concerned with her. At the moment it was more important to make this Zinochka, this sexy little secretary, conscious of her place in life and of my own inner worth.

A bitch available to any of the proofreaders and in

178

the daylight hours to the editor (who had the habit of slapping her bottom) having the nerve to teach me lessons! Slap her bottom indeed! As a person totally consecrated to the lofty cause of art I was completely free from such vulgar interests. But if I'd had the luck to get *In Search of Joy* printed I could have slapped her to my heart's content and she wouldn't have objected. What's more, she'd have been flattered. But that's not what I'd have done. I'd have thought up something else. First I would have invited her to the Arts Theater. Then, in a splendid light gray suit and to the bows of flunkeys, I would have weakened her with dry Georgian wine to the point of nearly losing consciousness. Next I take her by the arm in this weakened condition to a hotel where there is a luxury apartment waiting for a great writer at any hour of the day, and there on a fourposter bed I subject her to every imaginable kind of humiliating procedure. Not because it's a matter of great urgency to me, but just in the interest of justice. Then she'll realize who she's dealing with. Then she won't insult a man who is on an immeasurably higher level than she, but for the time being lacks the facilities to prove his superiority . . .

The leatherette-upholstered door was unexpectedly thrown open. Through it flew the retired colonel, with a white crew-cut on top of a bronze skull and a disproportionately large chest development. Various medals were attached to him—the Order of the Active Service Red Banner, the Order of Glory, and some others. You might meet a fellow like that on the street and it would never occur to you that he spent his spare time training himself in the novelist's art. But now he was covered with sweat and was letting off steam like an armored train while the editor's castrato tenor pursued him from the rear. "Study Chekhov! Turgenev! Leo Nikolayevich Tolstoy! . . ."

My lucky moment had come.

I got out of the armchair and, after swiftly smoothing the back of my neck, made a stealthy move toward the gap formed by the escaping colonel. About five yards combined with a little cool determination and the editor, who was sitting under cover, would have been in my hands. My first phrase, humorous in style, had already been prepared. The great thing in such cases is not to betray timidity, but to be nonchalant, dignified, and familiar . . .

But clearly it wasn't my lucky day. That faithful watchdog, the office janitor, had kept me under observation and rushed to cut me off. The leatherette barricade fell under Zinochka's control before I made it. The young secretary's well-developed body, ripe for shame, barred my path.

"Let me in! Let me in!" I shouted, hoping that the editor would hear us. "*In Search of Joy* can't have been turned down by anyone. I haven't had the manuscript returned. This is a misunderstanding, an absurd misunderstanding . . ."

No doubt I'd have prevailed against the silly bitch in the end. But, as ill luck would have it, at that moment the writer B. swept into the office in person.

He and I had started off together as members of the same literary circle. In those days everyone used to laugh at his babblings. He wrote worse than anyone, worse even than Galkin. And now—well, I ask you—graphomaniac B. was a celebrity, though he had completely written himself out in the meantime and I could find no comparisons to express his utter mediocrity.

He was wearing a splendid light gray suit and carried an ivory cane. His large, well-nourished snout, his big forehead and fat cheeks wafted cool contentment into the overheated atmosphere. But *I* had this bird pretty well summed up and was unable to bear with equanimity his presence which was banishing me from the room just as the sunlight banishes stars from the vault of the morning sky . . . morning horizon . . . I felt as if I were disappearing along with my rumpled trousers, dissolving in my sweat-impregnated socks, melting in the pale smile, which, in defiance of my conscious intentions, was timidly creeping onto my salty lips.

A bit more of this and, if I hadn't kept my wits about me, B. would have started a condescending conversation about my wife and children, and would have offered me a loan of fifty rubles for old time's sake. In order not to become completely eclipsed in his eyes, which were waiting patiently for me to turn and greet him, I had to beat a retreat. I remarked diplomatically, as if trying to recollect something, "Oh, another thing," I said. "Tell your boss I haven't time, Zinochka. I haven't time to talk to him today."

But her whole body was already drawn in the direction of the writer B. All her curls were nodding in welcome to him. I wouldn't look in the direction toward which she was yearning, and didn't turn my head . . .

When I was on the stairs a suspicious laugh reached my ears. Zinochka was giving a joyous squeak, as if she was being tickled. The lion's roar of the successful graphomaniac accompanied her in the bass. Soon they were joined by a third voice. That must be the editor who had emerged from his ambush and, slapping Zinochka on her back, twisted in a paroxysm of mirth, had himself gradually started to emit some feeble sounds . . .

I bit my left wrist in revenge for the humiliation they were causing me. A clear imprint of teeth emerged on the blue skin, shaped like a white necklace. In two or three of the indentations blood appeared.

This sharp pain made me feel better at once. I gave a sigh and thought that I would one day write a book in which I would paint that trio in satirical colors. Then they'd understand who they were dealing with; but it would be too late.

It was all right for the classical writers of the nineteenth century. They lived in quiet country houses, had fixed incomes, and in between magnificent dances and duels would sit on glass-protected verandas, writing novels that were immediately published in every corner of the globe. They knew some foreign language from the moment of their birth, were taught various literary devices and styles in *lycées*, traveled abroad where they reinforced their brains with fresh material—and as for their children, well, they just gave them to a governess to look after, and they sent their wives off to dances or to the dressmaker or shut them up in the country.

But just try it nowadays—try to evoke inspiration when your organism demands food and your head is oppressed with the thought of how to get to your essential goal and how to break through the barriers erected in your path by graphomaniac blackguards who have entered literature by means of a shady path, walling up all entrances and exits behind them. Where are you to get your three meals a day? Then there's the gas and electricity to pay for, the soles of your shoes are full of holes, and you have to settle with the typist for two hundred pages of typescript at a ruble a page . . .

What a miserable existence!

I look at myself and marvel. Can it really be that this brain of genius and this ardent, indomitable heart have been reared on rotten cutlets? I'm not exaggerating—rotten cutlets and nothing else all my life. And there's no glass veranda, there's no rudimentary desk, even, to write this sentence on, and, as I'm writing it, on the upper floor above my bowed neck some trumpeter is braying away on his trumpet, uninterruptedly practicing the same futile tune for five hours on end.

When writing *In Search of Joy* I used to plug my ears with cotton wool and wind a towel around myself. I would cover my eyes with the palm of my hand and work blindly so as not to see the depressing marks on the wall —traces of bugs and greasy patches—and, exerting my will power, would try to isolate myself from the kitchen smell and from the trumpetings that penetrated my consciousness through the cotton wool and towel. Now try comparing me with Leo Tolstoy or with Ivan Turgenev!

183

I don't know which of them, which of those classical writers, would agree to my proposal: let them print me and then let me fall ill and die immediately without properly tasting all my posthumous glory. Just publish only one book (preferably *In Search of Joy*) and then kill me or do what you like with me—I'll accept any ultimatum. But which of you would accept it; which of you would meet such conditions? . . .

My wife was not at home, having not yet returned from work. Little Paul was sitting apart, sitting on the bed with his legs dangling, drawing in his notebook. I invited him to choose a different place to draw and lay on the bed to rest from the heat and restore my nerves. Zinaida might arrive at any moment and I had a clear picture of myself giving her a piece of my mind, but I was also troubled by a certain problem: where had she hidden the package, addressed to me personally, which (without a word to me) she had concealed in my absence a week ago? I was all the more troubled because I did not possess a carbon copy, and this one was, so to speak, the sole specimen of the fullest version. How would I feel if I were suddenly to lose it?

Little Paul brought me out of my reveries. He rushed up to the head of the bed and silently deposited on my chest his notebook in which, on this occasion, something had been written.

In the previous month he had just managed to learn to write as a result of Zinaida's efforts, and I did not expect to find in the book a finished composition—the first (if I may so express it) story by my son, executed in even, printed, penciled letters. To avoid leaving any gaps, I shall quote the text in its entirety without changing a single word and only removing crude spelling mistakes.

Story

On a sunny day. Near a forest swamp where the grass grew very thickly, little spots were flashing. They were dwarfs, finger-sized. They wanted to make their town near the swamp. First they cut and sawed grass. The dwarfs were wrapped up in leaves. The dwarfs were divided into brigades. Second, they were gathering grass into piles. Third, they were weaving grass. Fourthly they were trampling down the earth. In a word, they were very busy.

"Did you make this up yourself?" I asked sternly.

Paul stood as if he had been screwed to the iron leg of the bed. He had a guilty smile on his lips and he did not speak. His pale little cheeks were blazing with the fire of immature ambition. It was not easy for me to plunge the surgeon's cold scalpel into his young soul, but I well understood my duty: to carry out the operation on the spot before it was too late, while he was still a child and would not feel it.

"It's an excellent thing that you can write," I said, casting a critical eye over his squiggles. "If you want to, copy the large print in newspapers, book titles, and the names of birds and animals. That will do no harm. But why write down all the rubbish that comes into your head?

Give me your word, Paul dear, never to do it again, never to make up any fairy tales about Lilliputians. That is stupid and shameful, and everyone will start laughing at you and teasing you if they find out . . ."

I tore the page with the story out of his notebook, and, ostentatiously crumpling it up, stuck it in my trouser pocket. His little face twisted, he swallowed silently and was working up to a howl.

"When you grow up, Paul dear, and read the fat works composed by your father, you will understand this is no simple matter and that what is needed here is talent, perhaps even genius. Just think—what will happen if everyone starts writing? Who's going to do the work, who will do the reading if there's no one around except writers? No, let's go halves. I'll be the writer, and you can be an engineer or a musician. Daddy's a writer and Paul's a pilot, Paul's a great general, a sailor—you know how much fun that is. 'Over seas, over waves, here today and there tomorrow.' "

I got up, walked around the room, and lay down on the bed again. How was one to explain the whole complexity of this situation to a child of six, still not old enough for school? Surely not by introducing him to the theory of probability and to the theory of heredity.

I will not conceal that in the first moment it had given me pleasure. After all, it was my own nature, my literary blood. It meant that I must be worth something if even my seed, scattered at the whim of fate, was sprouting in twisted letters on a child's drawing paper . . .

But I was well aware that writers do not beget writers

and that geniuses have no posterity. Leo Tolstoy's children did not have the right to be authors. The Dumas don't count. They're both worthless, especially Dumas *fils*. And Zinaida was stupid enough to call our son Paul. She never loved me. "Paul Straustin" on book covers and spines, on everyone's lips. Just try and sort out in two or three hundred years' time which of the two is me and which is he, the graphomaniac.

Moreover, what if one considers this point—do I love him, in the end, or don't I? My love for my son simply left me no alternative. There was the question of vicious habits in childhood. "The first step—a glass of wine, the last—a broken life." Must avert it! Yes, yes! For that reason alone. Be better for the boy himself . . .

"Do you hear, Paul? I forbid it. If you ever . . ."

Then, to console him, I told him that I would soon present him with a real typewriter. As soon as my book was published and we got terribly rich we would buy such a machine. Press a button and a letter flies out and makes an impression on the paper. All the letters, one after the other, and the punctuation marks. Almost like a book. Paul would learn to type, take a course in grammar, and learn to copy Daddy's manuscripts accurately —the trunkful of them that stands in the corridor and new ones, fresh from the pen. A typist costs money, lots of money. But Paul would take her place and our own family typist would appear in the house.

"Well, kiss your daddy. Please buck up and kiss Daddy!"

At the point of this kiss Zinaida arrived. While still

on the threshold she began to tell me off for lying on the clean bed in dusty boots while there was no bread, tea, sugar, or something else in the house. Then without getting up I asked her directly where the publisher's copy of *In Search of Joy* was and why she had said nothing about it before.

An argument started.

When I see Zinaida I find myself asking a question. Can it really be that this alien, elderly, ugly woman, worn out by women's diseases, dressed any old way and eternally hurrying off somewhere—can it be that she is my wife and how could this have come about? But after all ten years ago she had loved me and believed in my star, was entranced by every word which I created and used to say that the editors who didn't print me had no idea of art. It was, after all, her image, full of eagerness and passion, with streaming hair the color of ripe rye, which I had imprinted from memory in the image of Tatyana Krechet, altering only the name so that readers would not guess, and placing her in a different historical ambience. But now she was ready to tear my novel to pieces, having no interest whatever in my further plans as she spoke, sitting in a deliberately tired pose in her chair and twisting her thin leg in a drooping stocking with holes in it.

"It would be better if you were an alcoholic. Drug addicts are better. At least they do have lucid intervals. They love their wives and show fondness for their children. Not a scrap of attention do we get. Has time only for the arts. Butter. Four months without work. Support

188

the household myself. Doesn't see any meat. If your wife was unfaithful to you you wouldn't even notice it. Heartless lump of stone. There's no sugar left. Paul has anemia. Come here, Paul. Daddy doesn't love us. Come here."

Sniffling, Paul left my bed and made his way to the chair on which she was sitting, while I had the thought that it really would be a way out if Zinaida should suddenly be unfaithful to me with someone who would marry her. But who would have her—an ugly old woman with a six-year-old child and her stockings in holes? She'd be a stone around my neck till the day of her death. If she were to die it would be quiet and spacious in the room and it would be possible to write peacefully in the evenings. But Paul might as well live—he was a quiet, polite boy who wouldn't get in my way. When he grew up he would be entrusted with the whole of my archives, or even museum, as is the usual practice with the children of famous writers.

"Paul, come here! Why have you deserted me? Don't you love your daddy?"

He jumped off Zinaida's lap and obediently ran to the bed. While fondling his quivering, angular shoulder blades I told my wife that Stendhal too had been persecuted in his day, that my books would have repercussions perhaps in three hundred years' time and that she should immediately return the manuscript, which would in any case someday be read and appreciated, albeit too late.

Zinaida raged on her chair, sobbing and lamenting. "Paul, don't you dare listen to this person! Is this person really dearer to you than your mother? Come here at once! And you, Paul senior, are a maniac. You need treatment. You've got this obsession with becoming a historical figure. You haven't the courage to be an ordinary mortal. But you're a mediocrity, that's what you are! Oh dear, I'm so unhappy! . . ."

With a theatrical movement she struck her head against the plaster, thus deliberately causing a bruise, after which she set up an even more ringing yelp. Obviously you couldn't expect a kid of six to spot the fraud. He slid out of my embrace and popped up in her arms. My emotions also got the better of me and we began to shout at each other everything we'd been storing up, fighting for the affections of our son, who kept crossing over from one camp and one set of arms to the other.

"Paul, don't dare! Paul, come back! It's me, your mother! And I'm your father, your father! Come here, Paul! No, come here! Don't go to her! Don't go to him! Paul darling! Paul!"

He was running from the bed to the chair and back, hunched, silent, insignificant-looking. He darted about the room so quickly that there seemed to be a lot of dwarfs bustling around seriously with a great deal to do, as was described in the story of his own composition. Finally Zinaida threw her arms around him and wouldn't let him go. Hearing my appeals, he was struggling to escape from captivity, but he started to have hiccups and kept up a loud and frequent hiccupping without being able to stop.

"Now you see what you've brought him to!" hissed

Zinaida, as if it hadn't been her fault, and left the room, holding Paul firmly so that he wouldn't run away. But though she had forcibly seized my child, victory was partly on my side because on her way out she bent down and pulled from under a cupboard the precious manuscript that I had already given up for lost.

"There! I hope you choke on it!" she exclaimed, hurling it straight at me with a one-handed swing. *In Search of Joy* hit the back of the bed and the pages came loose and scattered. I rushed to pick them up.

So now it had returned to its creator, this book that had experienced so many misfortunes on the road to glory. It was smeared with dust, the pages were mixed up, and some of them (as I spotted immediately) were missing, while many were creased, torn, or disfigured from top to bottom by the editor's corrections in blue pencil. I picked page 167 at random and read: "By the edge of the abyss stood Tatyana Krechet, her golden hair, the color of ripe rye, streaming in the wind." In the margin opposite this sentence a question mark had been inscribed in blue pencil.

I sat on the floor and burst into tears and in my tears addressed myself to little Paul, who, as it seemed to my imagination, was still in the room.

"Now you understand why I forbade you to write stories? Do you understand now?"

Then, still crying, I said to Zinaida, "Let's agree that I am a graphomaniac. But whose business is that? Who suffers from it?"

But Zinaida had left long ago. I was alone, and luckily no one could observe my moment of weakness.

When I reached him just after midnight, with no luggage except a briefcase, Galkin was not yet going to bed.

"About time too! Either the family or one's art. Have to make the choice," he said, warmly supporting my idea of making a permanent break with Zinaida.

To my surprise his room turned out to be spacious and comparatively clean, but the things in it were disposed abnormally. There was a teapot on the floor, a table lamp too, while the table was occupied by a paperweight and all sorts of rubbish. On an electric stove some joiner's glue was heating in a shaving mug.

"You see, Paul Ivanovich, I'm setting up a bookbinder's workshop. As a relaxation and amusement. Books are the bane of my life . . ."

Galkin's books reached the ceiling and his shelves were bent like a bow. I pulled a book out automatically—Konstantin Fedin's *First Joys* and *An Unusual Summer*.

"Haven't read 'em!" said Galkin angrily. "And I'd advise you not to. In general, I'll tell you frankly, I hardly do read books. I write 'em. Why should we read when we're writers ourselves and can at any moment compose anything we want ourselves? . . . Come, look—"

He led me to a shelf where just a single section was covered with glass and took from behind the glass a book in a brightly colored cover. It was without a title and seemed quite new. Looking at the title page, I felt my heart sink:

Semyon Galkin
IN THE WHALE'S BELLY
His Nineteenth Book of Verse
Moscow, 1959

Instead of congratulating him I wanted to make a cutting remark. He must have bribed an editor to print his cockeyed ravings illicitly. But Galkin forestalled me, uttering in unconcealed triumph, "Look at the details of publication! What do you say about the size of the edition?"

On the back of the last page the following had been set up in small type: "Editor, S. Galkin. Artistic designer, S. Galkin. Technical editor, S. Galkin. Typesetter, S. Galkin. Size of edition—1 copy."

I slowly started to laugh. First diffidently, then—as I grasped the truth—noisily, affectionately, and wholeheartedly. It was a brilliant forgery. And though the feeling I had experienced caused my fingers to tremble, I turned the leaves from cover to cover and even smelled the paper. Without any concealment I expressed my delight to the author. I especially liked the commas, so tiny and exact—in a word, completely genuine commas.

"You ought to print forged currency! Your talent is going to waste," I said in jest and dug him in the ribs. "But tell me, Semyon, have you got your own printing press? How was this done?"

"Dilute India ink and water colors," Semyon answered gloomily, taking the unique copy of his book from me with incomprehensible speed. "Well, that'll do, friend. Let's go to bed."

I spent three days at Galkin's. He fed me on sandwiches and sausage and gave me as much sweet tea as I could drink. But his way of life interfered with my thoughts and distracted me from the complicated labor of repairing my manuscript. Systematically, one sentence after another, I called to mind and restored the text removed from my novel by the efforts of malignant persons, while Semyon, joking and chattering, was cooking up his translations.

"Stop wagging your tongue! Call yourself a writer?" I often said in indignation at his capacity for perpetually concocting every possible kind of nonsense.

But in this matter Galkin had his own lunatic arguments. By his lights the titanic labor of a writer consisted of conversation. The writer chatters with his friends, mulls it over in the rough, repeats hackneyed phrases, stumbles, talks drivel. And suddenly—he's caught it! Caught something that has strayed into his mind and tripped onto his tongue. And that's the vital thing: to blurt out some unexpected word in which from now on the whole world, as Galkin liked to say pompously, would see its true and most exact synonym.

From time to time he grew silent and would sit with his fat lips apart, motionless for fifteen minutes on end and looking like an idiot—just like a sheep or, to be more accurate, a ram. On such occasions I was angered by the damage done to my inspiration and by the fact that with his conversations or sudden trances he riveted my attention and prevented me from concentrating. Then I would drop some article on the floor—a pencil, some scissors, and once, for the sake of experiment, a heavy manuscript —*In Search of Joy*. Galkin did not react. From his protuberant lower lip a strand of spittle hung down onto his collar.

He was especially pathetic at night, when he would wake up and arouse me by his loud muttering, then, without his trousers on, would hurl himself at the table and, scratching his unwashed legs, scrawl page after page, tear it up into small pieces, and lurch into bed, reeling like a drunk. He used up a fair amount of paper in the daytime too . . .

"You know, friend," Galkin would say with a silly, broad grin, "the more work I do, the better I understand that my best compositions don't belong to me. Damn it, they don't seem to have been written by me at all. They just come into my head obliquely, flying in from the air. People talk about 'making one's mark,' 'expressing one's personality.' But in my opinion every writer is occupied by one thing alone: self-suppression. That's why we labor in the sweat of our brow and cover wagon loads of paper with writing—in the hope of stepping aside, overcoming ourselves, and granting access to thoughts from the air. They arise spontaneously, independently of ourselves. All we do is to work and work, and to go farther and farther along the road, mastering ourselves from time to time and giving way to them. Then suddenly —after all, it always is a sudden, immediate process— it becomes clear that you composed one thing yourself, so that it's worthless, while another thing is not yours and you don't dare, don't have the right to do anything with it, either to change it or to improve it. It's not your property! And you retreat in bewilderment. You're flabbergasted. Not at any particular beauty of the achievement. Simply from terror at your own non-participation in what has taken place . . ."

I listened carefully to Galkin's frank confessions. I even found them very interesting. So that's the way it was! Doesn't consider the stuff his own property? That must be taken into account . . . But then who is the composer? Whom does he borrow all this from? Events confirmed my worst fears.

Among the guests at Galkin's place certain persons of dubious appearance were often knocking about. They would turn up without ceremony, sit down without invitation. Everything about them made it clear that this house served them as a headquarters or as a transportation point on the winding routes of literature. On the first morning there arrived a female personage of about forty-eight or forty-nine, whose hair was close cropped like a boy's and who spoke of herself as if she were a man. She would refer to herself as "a fellow like me" or "this fellow."

"This fellow's brought a new play. Five-acter," she threw out offhandedly and held toward Galkin her left hand covered with peeling nail polish. Crossing her legs, canting her knee up to her chin and embracing it with crossed fingers, she smoked unceasingly, screwing up her eyes in the tear-provoking smoke and making a wry face as she rolled along her mouth a well-chewed cigarette of the cheap brand called Surf.

After her departure Galkin gave her a testimonial.
"A proofreader. Used to work on one of the serious monthlies. Got fired because of a political lapse. Writes detective plays. Sharply criticizes ministers and the top bureaucracy. Fails to get her stuff printed solely because of censorship conditions. Was the first wife of a well-known violin-player, a pansy . . ."

Then came the visit of a teacher of botany, a bald, anemic type with malachite cuff links and a kind, imbecile smile, the general favorite of older secondary-school girls. He spent a little over four hours with us—the two of them were sticking together a strange cardboard figure like a sea urchin. As Galkin later explained, this was a book (another book!), but one which opened up like a concertina and was covered inside with abstract verses. Other books—in the shape of a cube, a pyramid, and an egg—had been executed a month previously, again with the cooperation of Galkin, who saw in these articles a new synthesis of poetry, painting, and sculpture.

I wished to be rid of these uninvited guests and to help my host in this matter. What sense did it make for him to play Maecenas to every graphomaniac, mediocrity, and failure? He himself was a graphomaniac and a failure!

Galkin grew heated. "You don't understand a thing! You write vast novels about the Revolution and Civil War. How old were you in 1919? . . . And here, blazing under your nose, are passions worthy of a Shakespeare's brush . . . Shylocks, jaguars! Oh, if only I were a playwright!"

He cavorted around the room, shaggy, looking like a sheep erect on its hind legs and tripping over teapots and glasses that were disposed around the parquet as if it were a tablecloth. His stampings caused books to fall from the upper shelves, emitting puffs of dust, and he trampled the books underfoot, shouting threateningly at the ceiling, "Just you wait, Straustin! You'll see! We'll gather together—there'll be a full turnout . . . God, what people live in this Russia of ours! Live in vain and die uselessly . . ."

Soon I had the opportunity to observe this spectacle worthy of Shakespeare's brush. The place was jammed with a crowd of twenty, twenty-five, or thirty people. There weren't enough chairs. People were sitting on the window sills and on the *Encyclopedic Dictionary of Brockhaus and Efron.*

Here were representatives of all sects, generations, and movements. There were old ladies in Chekhovian pince-nez who wrote about pig farms, and there were youthful neophytes with Pushkinian curls whose work was in the manner of Yesenin. My old friend the retired colonel was also buzzing around, wearing all his medals. He had made contact with a fellow in a tattered sailor's vest. The boy smelled of liquor, prison, and suicide. He was shyly looking sideways at the more presentable of the crowd, and the colonel was encouraging him. "Drop it, Grisha! You'll be all right with me . . ."

Galkin was in charge of the assemblage. He felt as if it was his birthday and hardly had everyone sat down when he begged attention for what he called a few words of welcome.

"Go on! Go on!" cried the composer of detective plays.

"Go on!" burbled the botany teacher, imitating her, embarrassedly squeezing between his knees that specimen of synthesis, the model of a sea urchin.

"Dear colleagues! Comrades graphomaniacs!" began the speaker in a voice of thunder. Through the room spread a united mutter of indignation.

"And what do you think you are?" barked the retired colonel.

But this was just what Galkin was waiting for. He drew an analogy between a graphomaniac and a genius, thus calming the audience. He termed graphomania the foundation of foundations and the beginning of beginnings, calling it the swampy soil from which the springs of poetry draw their origins. This soil, Galkin said, is saturated with moisture. It can't escape, Galkin said. A time will come, said Galkin, when it will burst out of the bowels of the earth and flood the world. He who was nothing, said Galkin, will become everything, and even if there isn't enough paper for everyone we shall cover the walls of the houses and the bare pavements of the streets with texts in verse and prose, said Galkin.

The gathering responded with a sympathetic rustle. But I noticed that some impatience was manifesting itself among the graphomaniacs. They were going off into corners. Groups of two or three persons were forming and while one author was reading some composition of his own aloud the others were waiting, shifting from one foot to the other. They all had the urge. No one was listening to Galkin any more . . .

". . . above us a sky with a woman's smile and violet as the plum of the lieutenant called Greben was resting on the green grass. General Ptitsyn, not wiping away the few soldierly tears which were rolling down his cheeks, uttered the command: 'I love you, darling Tonya,' and their lips fused in a fiery kiss. And he sensed in his soul one of those pieces of curd tart and mushroom pies, and half a dozen strong pickles, cold as icicles and smelling of fresh dill after being salted away in early spring when one wants to join nature in weeping with joy and cry: 'O Russia! Whither art thou rushing?' while blessing the first downy, tender, pink snow to fall on the black, muddy, slippery road. The east was covered with a ruddy dawn and do you suppose, Vyacheslav, that the minister is unaware of that? The minister is shielding the criminals, but why, Vyacheslav, do you press my hand firmly and caress me with your gray eyes, yet without making any intimate approach?"

Now everyone was shouting out his own stuff. The assembly had disintegrated into groups, the groups into units, and the units into parts. Red, sweaty foreheads. Chaotic hair styles. Hands emphasizing an exclamation mark and producing a comma out of emptiness. A mad gesticulation of mouths full of foam and spittle, filling the air with crude noises.

"The combine harvester, the combine harvester, Nastya. The lime trees were in bloom not to gobble up amid the

golden cockerels. A frontier guard of crystal, moun-
taineers on a sailor's hat. Igor, raging, said nothing.
Deputy Minister of a silver-birch coppice. Hiccuts hic-
cuppery violets with emery paper. Inasmuch as they
plow the field with tractors. The secretary was sent for.
Secretary of the District Committee Lykhov feather-veined
on the Dnieper's dawn. Ham in the ground, the dawn
ahead. Ablaze, ablaze! Not surprisingly. Sneak in the
bosom. Arling, arling whatcha bootiful! Limes flowering.
Jasmine walrus far as the horizon. She pronounced in
parallels. 'Hurrah, fellows! Is Moscow not behind us?
So rhubarb on the captain!' "

Suddenly in the confusion there flashed a phrase which
made me start and turn around. Someone said, "The
breath of an approaching thunderstorm could be sensed
in the air . . ."

It flashed like lightning and drowned in the fog of the
words that swirled above me. Turning around impetu-
ously, I could not tell which of these babbling mouths had
just pronounced a quotation from my novel *In Search of
Joy*. But mistaken I could not be, for on only the previous
day had I inserted in the text the sentence about the approaching thunderstorm—in precisely that variant in
which it had been repeated here.

And then again, in confirmation of my hideous sur-
mise, another voice at the other end of the room quietly
but intelligibly said, "Brea . . . proach . . . orm . . .
ensed . . . air."

No doubt about it, I'd been robbed. My pearl had been
stolen.

Without delay I elbowed my way through to Semyon. He was contemplating the bacchanalia in the posture of a Napoleon. With his sunken nostrils and with his fat lips stretched as if to whistle, he was greedily drinking in all the words and sounds which were flying chaotically around the room. He was so absorbed by this activity that he didn't even notice me. And I at that moment—my eyes were opened, and with the clarity of an artist who has suddenly comprehended the full baseness of life, I read intuitively all that was written on Galkin's greedy face.

It was precisely he, Galkin, and none other who had been the main cause of my loss. Not for nothing had he on the previous day been disseminating that philosophy about how we allegedly compose nothing good ourselves and how the best thoughts enter our minds from the air. No accident either that he was now listening attentively to everything. Tomorrow he'd use it and say, "Not my property," "Came into my head accidentally, tripped onto my tongue." With the same casualness he had surrendered my golden pearl to his graphomaniac pals. Probably he'd spotted it in the manuscript while I was asleep or visiting the lavatory . . . And now it was passing from hand to hand like small change among cheats and scoundrels.

I caught Galkin by the sleeve and asked him spitefully, "Wouldn't you like to write it down, Semyon? So as not to forget it and use it tomorrow . . ."

"Yes!" he said, without even a blush. "I would! But you see, I'm not a playwright, and unfortunately not a writer of prose. I won't be able to bring it off . . . But in your place, Straustin, I'd compose something of the

kind . . . A short story—better still, a novella, a novel,
an epic! I'd call it *Graphomaniacs!* An epic about unsuccessful writers. The material, the material that's going
begging!"

Seeing that he was trying to dodge, I asked him, also
rather ironically, "And what do you think of this sentence,
Semyon? I just happened to hear it." And I quoted the
final chord from my novel: "The breath of an approaching thunderstorm could be sensed in the air."

But once again Galkin did not blush. "A poor sentence," he said coolly. "As hackneyed as an old twenty-
kopeck piece. But is that really the point? It isn't a question of how they write, but of how they yearn!"

There was no point in arguing with him. He pretended
not to catch my hints and began orating again. "Failures?
Everyone's a failure! Everyone's an unsuccessful genius!
But it's only we, we failures, who have comprehended the
full depth of our potentialities for genius, it's only we who
know . . . And it is in us, in us alone that humanity's
self-knowledge is to be found . . ."

Galkin was addressing everyone. But the graphomaniacs were in ecstasy. They were playing a game, juggling
with words and snatching the cards from each other, and
they didn't notice anything. My heart was filled with con-
tempt. They had stolen my treasure, called it a twenty-
kopeck piece, and put it in circulation to increase their
chances. It didn't help them. They were all losing, losing
desperately; they were literally ruining themselves before my eyes . . .

·   ·   ·

That night I couldn't sleep. I placed my stolen manuscript under my head to prevent Galkin from conducting any further depredations. Now I could uninterruptedly check its hard, yet not so hard, outlines with the back of my head during the night. I could see that I mustn't stay at Galkin's any longer.

My host was snoring with sublime calm on the top of the desk where he had rigged a bed out of books, an overcoat, and the only cushion in the house. On the ottoman where Galkin usually slept the botany teacher was stretched out. He had to be in school for the first class and was spending the night here instead of going home to Fili. His presence also brought me no joy. I moved the lamp toward the divan, and, seeing that I was in for a sleepless night anyway, took down Konstantin Fedin's *First Joys* and *Unusual Summer*.

The style seemed to me flabby and the subject dull. Like the majority of modern authors, who have turned literature into an impregnable fortress, Fedin possessed neither intelligence nor talent nor a knowledge of his subject. He was speaking of the Revolution and Civil War without having any understanding of these matters. But some words and expressions upon more attentive consideration stood out as superior and seemed to be quite familiar to me. Examining them carefully, I detected in them a close similarity to myself—to my books of various periods that had still not been published.

For example, Fedin wrote: "The road led to a spacious flower and vegetable plantation." And in my story of

1935, *The Sun Rises above the Steppe,* there was, as I well remembered, the sentence: "The road led to a spacious field planted with apple trees." Only my apple trees, as I remember, were in bloom, with pink petals glinting in the sunlight. But Fedin, in order to conceal his plagiarism, had liquidated all the beauty on my blossoming trees and had thereby made this scene immeasurably inferior. All the same the crumbs from my table, even in distorted form, had helped him rapidly to achieve a brilliant career, and now, without any qualms of conscience, he was consuming the fruits of glory which by rights belonged to me alone.

How I cursed my credulity! My manuscripts had remained in publishers' offices without getting any farther, only to return to me a month or more later with pages plucked and an invariable rejection. And while I was tormented by apprehensions the nimble fingers of various Galkins and Fedins were cunningly working over my stuff and launching it under the names, the false names, of other people . . .

I got out of bed and ransacked the shelves, collecting a pile of books published in recent years. And whatever book I looked at, after opening it in the middle, whether it was Leonov, Paustovsky, Fadeyev, or Sholokhov, everywhere I kept bumping into my own imprints, submerged in a mass of stupid and quite impossible text. Even in François Mauriac—on the most cursory examination— I found four details borrowed from a story of my youth called *Man,* and I spent ages racking my brains for the

205

explanation before hitting on the fact that, after all, the thieves could also have sent copies of my works abroad . . .

I was so shattered by all these impressions that toward morning I unexpectedly fell into a doze and had a nightmare. I dreamed that I was asleep and that a sheet of paper, speckled with typewriter marks, was, as it were, cutting its way into my skull case through the back of my head and cerebellum. I am looking at this paper with eyes turned around to the back of my head and struggling to read what is printed there—on which, it seems, all my personal fate hangs. But the blurred paragraphs keep emerging in front of me for a second and growing dim, then emerging and growing dim all over again, and I get nowhere. For a long time I suffered, still without making out what was printed there, and when I awoke, my head was numb and my neck ached and the clock read four in the afternoon.

The botany teacher had decamped, and Galkin, who was dressed, was sitting at the desk and rapidly writing something—probably everything he could remember of the previous day's claptrap. He was not inclined to conversation. His face was yellow, and to look at him closely was to undergo a repulsive experience.

I knew that I must get out of there quickly before the graphomaniacs had stripped me entirely, but for some reason I delayed and dawdled, loafed around from one corner to another, lay aimlessly on the sofa, kept stretching myself. It seemed to me that there was something I needed before I could get up and go. Feeling for a twenty-kopeck piece in my pocket, I went up to the glassed-in section where Galkin kept the books he had produced manually, and quietly tapped my twenty-kopeck piece against the protective pane. Galkin put up with it at first, then asked me to spare him, then raised his head and snarled, "Shut up! What do you want?"

I left him in peace for five minutes, then joined in the game again and methodically amused myself at his expense until he jumped up from the table and started cursing. Then I told him, as calmly as I could, "But my dear Galkin, you really are a graphomaniac. You're a really genuine, commonplace graphomaniac . . ."

My nerves were on edge and blood was flowing to my heart in spasms, but I spoke in an even and almost affectionate voice in order thereby to irritate and trouble him the more violently and prove to him by factual incontrovertibility that he was an ordinary graphomaniac, graphomaniac, graphomaniac, graphomaniac—as I annoyingly repeated, rapping the glass.

"But why are you angry, Semyon? It was you who called graphomania an honorable title . . . So why are you inconsistent, Graphomaniac Galkin?"

When he reached the limits of endurance and let out a full-throated yell telling me to get out, I was overcome by a feeling approaching satisfaction. Unhurriedly gathering together my things, I pronounced, being entirely within my rights in uttering this pronouncement: "So now you're throwing me out . . . First you rob me and now you throw me out."

But I embarked on no explanations of the nature of his

guilt toward myself because he wouldn't have understood
anything anyway. I only uttered an additional farewell
reproach directed against his graphomania and quickly
shut the door to prevent him from hitting me in case he
should throw a book after me . . .

I had come to his place at night, and it was late in the
evening when I left him. Having absolutely nowhere to
go, I wandered the streets, which were growing quiet, with
my briefcase under my arm and without any specific aim
in view. My body kept craving food and then rejecting the
idea, my headache kept passing and then returning with
redoubled force. As for money, I had not a penny apart
from the twenty-kopeck piece, and also I had nothing to
do. Having nothing to do, I took to looking through the
lighted windows in ground floors and basements, and
wherever the curtains weren't carefully drawn, the picture that revealed itself was the same everywhere.

It was late evening—the graphomaniac's favorite hour
—and in every hole accessible to my eyes someone was
writing. I had the impression that the town was seething
with writers, all of whom, great and small, were moving
their fountain pens over paper.

How many were there? For what publication and for
what purpose were they writing? Everywhere were libraries, reading rooms, and millions of volumes. In
private apartments, too, cupboards, bookstands and tables
were tightly jammed, reserves of books were accumulating
on window sills and hanging down from the ceiling. And
every day and hour were issued new pamphlets which no

one needed and no one read. But this army of obsession-
ists went on working . . .

I was not one of them. My fate was more bitter, but
more worthy. In the midst of this writing fraternity I was
perhaps the only true writer, whose works, albeit unacknowledged, had formed the foundation of literature and
constituted its most precious pages. Words from my
books, plundered and marketed by my successful contemporaries, now adorn the best specimens from the work
of the world's most famous authors. They are imitated;
they are copied. People themselves don't write, but copy
me, knowing nothing of the humble creator who is wander-
ing underneath their windows. Yes! I had not entered the
front door wearing a laurel wreath but had penetrated
their bodies and souls through food and air as poison
penetrates the blood, and now they would never be rid
of me . . .

The rows of illuminated windows grew noticeably
scarcer. The writers were going off to sleep. Soon only
isolated lamps were left in the houses, two or three to a
whole block. These were where the most vicious, diehard
graphomaniacs were persisting in their lunacy.

I was reeling and nauseated with exhaustion and fatigue. But I kept on and on without stopping, along Chekhov Street, along Gorky Street, over Pushkin Square . . .
And there were more streets named in honor of Leo
Tolstoy, Dostoyevsky, Mayakovsky, and either Lermontov
or Nekrasov. I did not walk among them, but I remembered that they existed.

The classical writers—it's them I hate most! Before I was so much as born they stole the vacant places and I was faced with their competition without possessing one hundredth part of their inflated authority. "Read Chekhov, read Chekhov!" people kept on at me all my life, tactlessly suggesting that Chekhov wrote better than I . . . And how could one fight against them when at Yasnaya Polyana even the nails of Leo Tolstoy, cut a thousand years ago and collected by some farsighted count in a special little bag, are preserved like a holy relic? And it's said that in Yalta, Chekhov's dried-up spit has been collected in special little packets—yes, the actual spit of Anton Pavlovich Chekhov, who is said to have suffered a great deal from the spitting of blood and even died of tuberculosis, which is of course a great exaggeration.

But to be honest, did Tolstoy and Chekhov really write so very well? Well, that's exactly my point! That Chekhov ought to be taken by his wretched tubercular beard and have his nose shoved in his consumptive hawkings that have unfortunately now dried up. "Stop writing, graphomaniac!" he ought to have been told. "Stop writing! Don't spoil good paper!"

But how can you? People will be found to defend him—admirers, bibliographers, memoirists. But who's going to write memoirs about me? Who, I ask you, will remember and immortalize me?

Being tired and upset, I was lurching on my feet, tottering and swaying. My difficult path along the street was whimsical and zigzag-shaped. It suddenly seemed to me that I wasn't walking along the street myself, but being guided by someone's fingers as a pencil is guided over paper. I was walking in small uneven script, following as hurriedly as I could the movement of the hand that was composing and noting down on the asphalt these deserted streets, these houses with windows here and there in which the lights had not been extinguished, and me myself, my whole long, long, unsuccessful life.

Then I snapped out of it, braked fiercely, and halted in full flight. I almost fell over and looked frowningly at the dark sky that hung low above my forehead. Addressing myself in that direction, I said softly but weightily enough, "Hey, you there—the graphomaniac! Stop work! All your writings are worthless. How feeble all your compositions are. You're unreadable . . ."

It was seven o'clock in the morning, but Zinaida was already up and was feeding little Paul on semolina. When she saw me she went wild with delight, pinched my head in both arms, bent it toward her, and gave it a hearty kiss. I tottered and sat down.

"I knew you'd come back— I knew it— I knew it—" she kept on, panting and pressing my face to her side. "You are kind, you are clever, you are generous. You understand, you understand at last . . . Oh, Paul, Paul!—"

I carefully freed my head from these embraces, and in order to afford Zinaida pleasure, gave her a smacking kiss on her rough hand. She uttered a sob. "And you really have come back for good? . . . You won't go away again? . . . We won't quarrel any more? . . . Yes? Yes?"

I had neither strength nor wish to refuse her, so I answered, "Yes."

"Yes!" I said, not very happily, but quite frankly. "I've made a decision. It's time to give the thing up. I'm not going to be a writer. It doesn't matter. I'll get along without it. I'll get a job, bring up little Paul . . . It's all right."

She fussed around me as if I were a celebrity. She gave me a clean towel, and a glass of milk normally destined for the child was solemnly handed to me—to help put my health to rights.

"You don't look well," Zinaida said in distress. "And your eyes somehow look dull . . . But never mind, never mind, now everything's behind you."

She promised me a new life starting that day and said that our home would now be full of light and joy, that we'd go to the theaters and movies; and, in order to leave me with some sort of male eccentricities, she gave me permission to buy a gun for hunting or, even better, to take up fishing if I wanted to. At worst she conceded that I might go in for occasional drinking, as I did sometimes in the days of my youth.

"All right, all right. You'll be late for work," I reminded her, giving her a kindly pat on the bottom. Zinaida's ugly face wrinkled in a smile. I even got the impression that she had grown pretty.

When she'd gone to work, little Paul and I gave the

dishes the once-over and swept the crumbs from the oil-cloth on the table.

"Now tell me, Paul, how are you and what are you composing?" I asked him point-blank, but in a cheerful voice.

Paul lowered his eyes and said nothing.

"Don't be afraid. I've changed my mind. Now you can write as much as you like. I won't take it away. Everything I said then was a joke. Here, take this—"

I found a piece of paper in my pocket, smoothed it out, and gave it to my son. The pencil marks were fading, but it was still possible to make out the letters. "You can make a neat copy of it. Sit down over here and write."

Paul climbed briskly under the bed for his notebook. Nine o'clock struck. The noise of a trumpet was heard from the floor above. It was the tenant upstairs who'd scarcely woken up and was beginning his first trill.

I also got a pile of clean paper out of my briefcase. I settled myself opposite Paul, spreading a newspaper over the oilcloth so the pages wouldn't stick. "Be sure not to tell your mother!"

I didn't want to deceive her and break the promise I had made. I had honestly promised to end the writing craze from which we had all suffered so long. And I definitely do intend to finish with it as soon as I've written my last work—my swan song. For many years I've been expecting this and have been drawing near it. A swan song about myself. No, no, not for print. Just let my son read it if he wants. And with that I'll have finished . . .

Paul was already copying the blurred squiggles.

"Write, Paul, write! Do not fear. Let them laugh at you and call you a graphomaniac. They're graphomaniacs themselves. There are graphomaniacs on all sides. There are many of us, many more than there should be. We live in vain and die uselessly. But one of us will make it. Either you or I or someone else. He'll make it, he'll get his message through. Write, Paul, compose your fairy tales about ridiculous dwarfs. And I'll write about mine . . . You and I will make up so many fairy stories —too many to count. Only be careful—don't say anything to Mother."

The trumpeter above my head was thundering away at full volume as if he wanted to hinder me. But my brain was as nimble as after a long sleep and my soul was full of inspiration. I took a fresh sheet and wrote on the top in capitals the title:

GRAPHOMANIACS

Then I thought for a moment and added in brackets:

(A Story from My Life).

1960

PKHENTZ

I MET him at the laundry again today. He pretended to be completely taken up with his dirty washing and unaware of me.

First came the sheets which people here use for reasons of hygiene. Along one edge of every sheet they stitch in tiny letters the word "FEET." This is by way of precaution against one's lips touching any part which the soles of one's feet may have rubbed and contaminated the night before.

Similarly a kick is considered more insulting than a blow with the hand, and not just because the foot hurts more. The distinction is probably a sign that Christianity still lives on: the foot must be wickeder than the rest of the body for

217

the simple reason that it is farther from heaven. Only the sexual organs are treated with less respect, and here there is some mystery.

Next came pillowcases with dark impressions in the middle. Then towels, which unlike pillowcases get dirtier round the edges, and, last of all, a colorful bundle of crumpled personal linen.

At this point he started tossing his stuff in at such a rate that I couldn't take a good look. Either he was afraid of giving away a secret, or else he was ashamed, as people always are, to exhibit objects directly pertaining to his legs.

But it was suspicious, I thought, that he had worn his clothes so long without getting them laundered. Ordinarily hunchbacks are clean. They are afraid that their clothes may make them still more repulsive. But this one, surprisingly, was such a sloven that he wasn't like a hunchback at all.

The woman who checked the laundry had seen everything. The marks left by the rarest of juices were old acquaintances to her. But even she couldn't help saying quite loudly: "What are you shoving it under my nose for, citizen? If you can't sleep properly, do your own laundry!"

He paid his money without a word and rushed out. I didn't follow him, because I didn't want to attract attention.

At home things were as usual. The minute I got into my room Veronica appeared. She bashfully suggested that we should have supper together. It was a bit awkward for me to say no to the girl. She's the only one in the apartment who treats me decently. It's a pity that her sympathy is grounded in sexual attraction. I'm absolutely convinced of this after what happened today.

"How's Kostritskaya?" I asked, steering the conversation on to common enemies.

"Oh, Andrei Kazimirovich, she's been making threats again."

"What's wrong?"

"The same as before. Light on in the bathroom and the floor all splashed. Kostritskaya informed me that she's going to complain to the superintendent."

The news infuriated me. I make less use of the plumbing than any of the others. I hardly ever go into the kitchen. Can't I make up for it by using the bathroom?

"Well, let her get on with it," I answered sharply. "She burns light by the kilowatt herself. And her children broke my bottle. Let the superintendent come."

But I knew very well that an appeal to the authorities would be a very risky business for me. Why draw attention to myself unnecessarily?

"Don't upset yourself, Andrei Kazimirovich," said Veronica. "I'll look after any trouble with the neighbors. Please don't upset yourself."

She put out her hand to touch my forehead, but I managed to dodge. "No, no, I'm quite well, I haven't got a temperature. Let's have supper."

Food stood on the table, steaming and stinking. The sadism of cookery has always amazed me. Would-be chickens are eaten in liquid form. The innards of pigs are stuffed with their own flesh. A gut that's swallowed itself garnished with stillborn chickens—what else, when you think of it, is scrambled egg with sausage?

Wheat is treated more unmercifully still: they cut it, beat it, crush it to dust.

"Eat up now, Andrei Kazimirovich," said Veronica coaxingly. "Please don't let it worry you. I'll take the blame for everything."

What about preparing a man to the same recipe? Take an engineer or writer, stuff him with his own brains, place a violet in one braised nostril, and dish him up to his colleagues for dinner. Yes, the torments of Christ, Jan Hus, and Stenka Razin are a bagatelle compared with the agonies of a fish jerked out of water on a hook. They at least knew what it was all for.

"Tell me, Andrei Kazimirovich, are you very lonely," asked Veronica, coming back with the teapot. When she had gone to fetch it I had emptied my plate into a sheet of newspaper.

"Did you ever have any friends"—she put in sugar—"or children"—another spoonful—"or a woman you loved?" . . . stir, stir, stir.

It was easy to see that Veronica was agitated.

"You are all the friends I need," I answered cautiously. "And as for women, you can see for yourself: I'm old and humpbacked. Old and humpbacked," I repeated with ruthless insistence.

I honestly wanted to forestall a declaration of love: things were difficult enough without it. It wasn't worth spoiling our alliance against the spiteful neighbors by rousing this unattached girl to a keener interest in myself.

220

To avoid trouble I thought of pretending to be an alcoholic. Or a criminal. Or perhaps better still a madman, or even a pederast? But I was afraid that any one of these roles would lend my person a dangerous fascination.

All I could do was to dwell on my hump, my age, my wretched salary, my humble job as a bookkeeper, and all the time it took up, to insist that only a woman with a hump to match would be right for me, whereas a normal, beautiful woman needed a symmetrical man.

"No, you are too noble," Veronica decided. "You think of yourself as a cripple, and you're afraid of being a burden. Don't think it's pity on my part. It's just that I like cactus, and you are like a cactus. What a lot of them you've got growing there on your windowsill!"

Her hot fingers touched my hand. I jumped as if I'd been scalded.

"You're freezing—are you ill?" asked Veronica anxiously. She was puzzled by my body temperature.

This was too much. I pleaded a migraine and asked her to leave me.

"Till tomorrow," said Veronica, waving her hand like a little girl. "And you can give me a cactus for a present tomorrow. I know you will."

This gentle girl talked to me like a head bookkeeper. She declared her love for me and demanded a reward.

Didn't I read somewhere that people in love are like humble slaves? Nothing of the kind. A man only has to fall in love to feel himself lord and master, with the right to boss anyone who doesn't love him enough. How I wish that nobody loved me!

When I was alone I set about watering my cacti from an enamel mug. I fed them slowly, my little humpbacked children, and relaxed.

It was two o'clock in the morning, when, faint from hunger, I crept on tiptoe along the dark corridor to the bathroom. But what a splendid supper I had then!

It isn't at all easy, eating only once a day.

That was two weeks ago. Since then Veronica has informed me that she has two beaus: a lieutenant and an actor at the Stanislavsky Theater. But it hasn't stopped her showing her predilection for me. She has threatened to shave her head so that I can't keep saying how stupid it would be to sacrifice her beauty to an old freak. Now she has got around to spying on me, lying in wait for me on the way to the bathroom.

"Cleanliness makes hunchbacks handsome"—that's my stock answer when she keeps asking why I take so many baths.

Just in case, I have started blocking up the frosted window between the bathroom and the lavatory with a piece of plywood. I always try the bolts before undressing. I couldn't stand the thought of somebody watching me.

Yesterday morning I wanted to fill my fountain pen, to continue my irregular diary, so I knocked at her door. Veronica wasn't up yet. She was reading *The Three Musketeers* in bed.

"Good morning," I said politely. "You'll be late for your lecture."

She closed her book. "Do you know," she said, "that the whole house thinks I'm your mistress?"

I said nothing, and then something horrible happened. Veronica, her eyes flashing, threw back the counterpane, and her whole body, completely uncovered, stared up at me angrily. "Look what you've turned down, Andrei Kazimirovich!"

Fifteen years ago I came across a textbook on anatomy. I wanted to know what was what, so I studied carefully all the pictures and diagrams. Later on, I had an opportunity of watching little boys bathing in the river at the Gorky Park of Culture and Rest. But, as it happened, I had never seen a naked woman in the flesh and at such close quarters.

It was—I repeat—horrible. I found that her whole body was of the same unnatural whiteness as her neck, face, and hands. A pair of white breasts dangled in front. At first I took them for secondary arms, amputated above the elbow. But each of them terminated in a round nipple like a push button.

Farther on, and right down to her legs, the whole available space was occupied by a spherical belly. That is where the food swallowed in the course of a day collects in a heap. Its lower half was overgrown with curly hair like a little head.

The problem of sex, which plays such a major role in their intellectual and moral life, had long troubled me. For safety's sake, I suppose, it has been wrapped from ancient times in a veil of impenetrable secrecy. Even the textbook on anatomy has nothing to say on the subject, or says it so vaguely and cursorily that no one can guess what it truly means.

So now, overcoming my confusion, I decided to take advantage of the opportunity, to take a look at the place

223

mentioned in the anatomy textbook as the site of that
genital apparatus which shoots out ready-made infants
like a catapult.

I caught a glimpse of something resembling human
features. Only it didn't look female to me, but more like
an old man's face, unshaven and baring its teeth.

A hungry, angry man dwelt there between her legs.
He probably snored at night, and relieved his boredom
with foul language. This must explain woman's dual nature, of which the poet Lermontov has aptly said:

> Fair as an angel of heaven,
> As a fiend cruel and false.

There was no time to work the thing out, because Veronica suddenly shuddered and said:

"Come on!"

She shut her eyes and opened her mouth, like a fish
pulled out of water. She thrashed about on the bed like
a great white fish, helplessly, vainly, and bluish goose
pimples covered her body.

"Forgive me, Veronica Grigorievna," I said timidly.
"Forgive me," I said, "it's time for me to go to the office."

And I tried to tread lightly and not to look back as I
went away.

It was raining outside, but I was in no hurry. It was
cleaning day in the department. I had escaped from Veronica, pleading official business (the estimates, the ni-
cotine, Head Bookkeeper Zykov, those crazy typists—

all for 650 rubles a month), and now I could afford the great luxury of a walk in the open in wet weather.

I found a leaky drainpipe and stationed myself under the stream. It ran right down my neck, cool and delicious, and in about three minutes I was damp enough.

The people hurrying past, all of them with umbrellas and rubber soles, looked at me sideways, intrigued by my behavior. I had to change my position, so I took a stroll through the puddles. My shoes were letting water in nicely. Down below, at least, I was enjoying myself.

"Oh Veronica, Veronica," I repeated indignantly. "Why were you so cruel as to fall in love with me? Why weren't you just the least bit ashamed of your appearance, why did you behave with such ruthless candor?"

Shame, after all, is man's fundamental virtue. It is a dim realization that he is irredeemably ugly, an instinctive dread of what he hides under cloth. Only shame, shame, shame can lend him a certain nobility, make him not of course more beautiful but at least more modest.

Needless to say, when I got here I followed the general fashion. You must observe the laws of the country you're compelled to live in. And anyway the constant danger of being caught, of being found out, made me force my body into this fancy dress.

But in their place I wouldn't shed my fur coat, let alone my suit, not even at night. I would find a plastic surgeon to shorten my legs and at least put a hump on my back. Hunchbacks are certainly a bit better-looking than the rest of them here, though they are monsters too.

Dejectedly I made my way to Herzen Street. My hunchback lodged there in a semi-basement opposite the Conservatoire. For six weeks now I had had my eye on this gracefully vaulted person who was so unlike a human being, and reminded me somehow of my lost youth.

I had seen him three times at the laundry and once in a flower shop, buying a cactus. I had been lucky enough to find out his address from a receipt which he had tendered to the laundress.

The time had come to dot the *i's*.

I told myself that it was impossible, that they had all perished and that I was the sole survivor, like Robinson Crusoe. Why, I had liquidated, with my own hands, all that was left after the crash. There were no others here but me.

But what if they'd sent him to look for me? Pretending to be a hunchback, in disguise . . . They hadn't forgotten me! They'd realized what had happened and mounted a search!

But how could they know? After thirty-two years. By local time, but still. Alive and well. That was quite something.

But why here precisely? That was the question. Nobody had meant to come here. Quite a different direction. It couldn't happen. We missed our way. Back of beyond. Seven and a half months. Then it happened.

Perhaps it was accidental. Exactly the same mistake. A deviation from course and the winter timetable. Any port in a storm. Do coincidences happen? Alike as two peas. Where none had set foot. It can happen, can't it? Disguised as a hunchback. Exactly like me. Even if there were only one, exactly like me!

The door was opened by a lady like Kostritskaya. Only this Kostritskaya was bigger and older. She exuded a smell of lilac, ten times normal strength. Perfume, that was.

"Leopold will be back soon. Come in, please."

An unseen dog was barking at the other end of the corridor. It couldn't make up its mind to spring at me. But I had had nasty experiences with animals of this kind.

"What's wrong? She won't bite. Down, Niksa, quiet!"

We wrangled politely while the animal raged, and three heads emerged from side doors. They looked me up and down with interest and cursed the dog. The din was awful.

I got through to the room, at great risk, and found there a small child armed with a saber. When he saw us he asked for berries and sugar and set up a yell, wriggling and pulling faces.

"He's a sweet tooth. Just like me," Kostritskaya explained. "Stop whining, or this man will eat you."

To please my hostess, I said jokingly that for soup I drank children's blood, warmed up. The child was quiet at once. He dropped his saber and cowered in the far corner. He didn't take his eyes off me. They were full of animal terror.

"Is he like Leopold?" the Kostritskaya asked, as though casually, but with a hoarse tenderness in her voice.

I pretended to believe the innuendo. The stale air, laced with the exhalations of lilac, made me feel sick. The smell irritated my skin, and a rash broke out in several places. I was afraid that my face might come out in green spots.

I could hear the savage Niksa scratching the corridor floor with her claws, and sniffing my tracks with a noisy snuffle. The excited lady lodgers, unaware of my heightened aural sensitivity, were conversing in half-whispers. "Anybody can see he's Leopold Sergeevich's brother . . ."

"No, you're wrong, our hunchy is Pushkin's twin compared to this one."

"Hope to God I never dream of anything like that . . ."

"Makes you feel funny just to look at him . . ."

All this was interrupted by Leopold's arrival. I remember that I liked the way he plunged straight into his part—the classic part of the hunchback who meets a monster like himself in the presence of third parties.

"Aha, a companion in misfortune! With whom have I the honor . . . To what am I indebted . . ."

He was copying a psychological pattern as fine-spun as a spider's web, pride protected by self-mockery, shame hiding itself in buffoonery. He mounted his chair like a horseman, gripping the seat between his legs, jumping up and sitting down again back to front, resting his head on the chair back, pulling weird faces, and continually shrugging his shoulders as though feeling the hump that loomed over him like a rucksack.

"Yes, yes. So you're Andrei Kazimirovich. And my name, funnily enough, is Leopold Sergeevich. As you can see I'm a bit of a hunchback too."

I was delighted with this skillful caricature of humanity, this art which was all the more natural because it was so absurd, and I realized rather sadly that he was my superior at the game of living, that I lacked his ability to enter into the only form of being possible for us on earth . . . that of hunchbacked monsters and injured egotists.

But business is business, and I gave him to understand that I wished to talk to him—*confidentially.*

"I don't mind going," said Kostritskaya huffily, and gave me a farewell gust of her caustic aroma as she left the room.

I revenged myself with the thought that she was saturated through and through in this smell. Even her excrement must smell of perfume, instead of boiled potatoes and home comforts, as is usually the case. She must piss pure eau de Cologne. In this atmosphere poor Leopold would soon wither away.

When we were alone, except for the petrified child sitting in the far corner with a dazed look of horror and mystification on his face, I asked him straight out:

"How long since you left?"

"Left where?" he answered evasively.

Our hostess's departure had wiped the assumed merriment from his face. Not a trace of that clownish exhibitionism found in most hunchbacks, who are clever enough to hide their spines and proud enough not to suffer because of it. I thought that he hadn't pulled himself together yet, and that from inertia he was wearily keeping up the pretense of being something other than his true self.

"Cut it out," I said quietly. "I recognized you at first sight. You and I come from the same place. We're relatives, so to speak. PKHENTZ! PKHENTZ!" I whispered, to remind him of a name sacred to us both.

"What did you say? . . . You know, I thought there was something rather familiar about you. Where could I have seen you before?"

He rubbed his brow, frowned, twisted his lips. The mobility of his face was almost human, and again I envied his extraordinarily well-rehearsed technique, although these cautious habits were beginning to irritate me.

"Of course!" he exclaimed. "Didn't you work once in the Stationery Supplies set-up? The director there in 'forty-four was Yakov Solomonovich Zak—such a nice little Jew . . ."

"I don't know any Zak," I answered curtly. "But I know very well that you, Leopold Sergeevich, are not Leopold Sergeevich at all, and no hunchback, although you keep flourishing your hump all over the place. We've had enough of pretenses now. After all, I'm taking just as big a risk as you are."

It was as though the devil had got into him:

"How dare you tell me who I am? Spoiling my relations with the landlady, and then insulting me as well! Go and find yourself a gorgeous woman like that," he said, "and then you can discuss my physical defects. You're more of a hunchback than I am! You're more disgusting. Monster! Hunchback! Wretched cripple!"

Suddenly he burst out laughing and clapped his hand to his head: "Now I remember! I've seen you at the laundry. The only resemblance between us is that we got our clothes washed in the same place."

This time I didn't doubt his sincerity. He really did think that he was Leopold Sergeevich. He had entered too fully into his part, gone native, become human, over-adjusted to his surroundings, surrendered to alien influences. He had forgotten his former name, betrayed his distant homeland, and unless somebody helped him he was as good as lost.

I grabbed him by his shoulders and shook him carefully. I shook him, and implored him in a gentle, friendly way to remember, to make an effort and remember, to return to his true self. What did he want with that Kostritskaya, who oozed such a poisonous odor? Even among humans bestiality was not respectable. And besides, betrayal of the homeland, even without malice aforethought, even out of ordinary forgetfulness . . .

"PKHENTZ! PKHENTZ!" I said over and over again, and repeated other words which I still remembered.

Suddenly an inexplicable warmth reached me through his Boston jacket. His shoulders were getting hotter and hotter, as hot as Veronica's hand, and thousands of other hot hands which I have preferred not to shake in greeting.

"Forgive me," I said, relaxing my hold. "I think there's some mistake. A regrettable misunderstanding. You see,

I—how can I explain to you?—I'm subject to nervous attacks . . ."

Just then I heard a terrible row and turned round. The child was dancing about behind me, at a respectful distance, and threatening me with his saber.

"Let Leopold alone!" he shouted. "Nasty man! Let Leopold alone! My mommy loves him. He's my daddy, he's my Leopold, not yours!"

There could be no doubt about it. I had mistaken my man. He was a normal human, the most normal of humans, hunchback or not.

I feel worse every day. Winter has arrived—the coldest season in this part of the world. I never put my nose out of the house.

Still, it's a sin to grumble. I retired on pension after the November holiday. I don't get much, but it's less worrying this way. How should I have managed otherwise during my last illness? I shouldn't have had the strength to dash to the office, and getting a doctor's note would have been awkward and dangerous. I wasn't going to submit to medical examination in my old age. It would have been the end of me.

Sometimes I ask myself a tricky question: why shouldn't I, after all, legalize my position? Why have I spent thirty years pretending to be somebody else, like a criminal? *Andrei Kazimirovich Sushinski. Half-Polish, half-Russian. Aged 61. Disabled. Not a Party member. Bachelor. No relatives, no children. Never been abroad.*

Born at Irkutsk. Father: clerk. Mother: housewife. Both died of cholera in 1901. And that's it!

But what about going to the police, apologizing, and telling the whole story simply, explaining it all just as it happened?

Well then, I'd say, it's like this. You can see for yourselves—I'm a creature from another world. Not from Africa or India, not even from Mars or one of your Venuses, but from somewhere still more remote and inaccessible. You don't even have names for such places, and if you spread out all the star maps and charts in existence before me, I honestly couldn't show you where that splendid point of light, my birthplace, has got to.

In the first place, I'm not an expert on astronomical matters. I went where I was taken. And in the second place, the picture's quite different, I can't recognize my native skies from your books and maps and things. Even now, I go out into the street at night, look up and there it is again—all wrong. I don't even know in which direction to yearn. It may be that not even my sun, let alone my earth, can be seen from here. It may be one of those on the other side of the galaxy. I can't work it out.

Please don't think that I came here with some ulterior motive. Migration of peoples, war of the worlds, and all that rot. Anyway, I'm not a military man, nor a scientist, nor an explorer. Bookkeeping is my profession—my profession here, that is. What I did before is best not mentioned. You wouldn't understand if I did.

In fact we had no intention of flying into space. To put it crudely we were going to a holiday resort. Then, on the way, something occurred—let's say it was a meteorite to make it easier for you—well then, we lost buoyancy and down we fell, into the unknown, for seven and a half months we went on falling—our months, though, not yours—and by pure chance we landed up here.

When I came to and looked around—all my fellow travelers were dead. I buried them in the prescribed way, and started trying to adapt myself.

Everything around was exotic and unfathomable. A moon was burning in the sky, huge and yellow—but only one moon. The air was wrong, the light was wrong, and all the gravities and pressures were strange. What can I say? The most elementary pine tree affected my otherworldly senses as a porcupine affects you.

Where could I go? I had to eat and drink. Of course, I'm not a man and not an animal; I incline more to the vegetable kingdom than to anything else you have here; but I too have my basic needs. The first thing I need is water, for want of a better form of moisture, and preferably at a certain temperature, and now and then I want the missing salts added to my water. And besides I felt a growing chill in the surrounding atmosphere. I don't have to tell you what Siberian frosts are like.

There was nothing for it, I had to leave the forest. For some days past I'd been looking at people from behind the bushes, sizing them up. I realized at once that they were rational creatures; but I was afraid to begin with that they might eat me. I draped myself in a bunch of rags (this was my first theft, and it was pardonable in the circumstances) and came out of the bushes with a look of friendship written all over me.

The Yakuts are a trusting and hospitable people. It was from them that I acquired the simplest human habits. Then I made my way to more civilized regions. I learned the language, obtained an education, and taught arithmetic in a secondary school in the town of Irkutsk. I resided in the Crimea for a time, but soon left because of the climate: it's oppressively hot in summer, and not warm enough in winter, so that you still need a room with radiators, and conveniences of that sort weren't too common there in the 'twenties and cost a lot of money, more than I could manage. So I made my home in Moscow, and I've been here ever since.

If I were to tell this sad tale, no matter to whom, no matter how skillfully edited for the general reader, nobody would believe me, not at any price. If I could only cry as my story requires. But though I've learned to laugh after a fashion I don't know how to weep. They'd think I was a madman, a fantasist, and what's more they might put me on trial for having a false passport, forging signatures and stamps, and other illegal activities.

And if, against all reason, they did believe me it would be worse still.

Academics from all the academies everywhere would flock in—astronomers, agronomists, physicists, economists, geologists, philologists, psychologists, biologists, microbiologists, chemists, and biochemists, to study me down to the last spot on my body, omitting nothing. They would be forever questioning, interrogating, examining, extracting.

Theses, films, and poems about me would circulate in millions of copies. Ladies would start wearing green lipstick and having their hats made to look like cactus, or failing that like rubber plants. For years to come all hunchbacks would enjoy enormous successes with women.

Motor cars would be called after my homeland, and after me hundreds of newborn infants, as well as streets and dogs. I should become as famous as Leo Tolstoy, or Gulliver, or Hercules. Or Galileo Galilei.

But in spite of this universal interest in my humble person nobody would understand a thing. How could they understand me, when I myself am quite unable to express my inhuman nature in their language. I beat about the bush and try to make some headway with metaphors, but when it comes to the point I can find nothing to say. I can only see a short, solid GOGRY, hear a rapid VZGLY-AGU, and an indescribably beautiful PKHENTZ beams down upon my trunk. Fewer and fewer such words remain in my memory. I can convey their structure only approximately in human speech. If I were surrounded by linguists asking "what do you call this" I could only shrug my shoulders and say: GOGRY TUZHEROSKIP.

No, I'd better put up with living lonely and incognito. If anything as special as me turns up it should exist unnoticed. And die unnoticed.

236

But then, when I die they may put me in a glass jar, pickle me in alcohol, and exhibit me in a Natural History Museum. And the people filing past will shiver with horror and laugh insultingly to cheer themselves up, and say with a grimace of disgust: "Heavens, how abnormal, what an ugly freak!"

I'm not a freak, I tell you! Just because I'm different do you have to be rude? It's no good measuring my beauty against your own hideousness. I'm handsomer than you, and more normal. Every time I look at myself I have the evidence of my own eyes for it.

Just before I fell ill the bath was cracked. I found out about it late one evening and realized that Kostritskaya had done it to vex me. I couldn't expect any help from poor Veronica. Veronica had been offended with me ever since the occasion when she offered me what was, humanly speaking, her most valuable possession, and I'd gone for a walk instead.

She has married the actor from the Stanislavsky, and sometimes the sound of their ethereal kisses wings to my ears through the thin wall. I was genuinely glad, for her sake, and on their wedding day I went so far as to send them an anonymous cake, with her initials and some arabesques executed in chocolate.

But I was incredibly hungry, and Kostritskaya had damaged the bath to destroy me, and, pending repairs, the hole where the water ran out had been stopped up with a wooden bung, and the water turned off. So when everybody had gone to bed and I could hear snores from the floor above and the floor below and all the rooms either side, I took Veronica's washtub off its nail in the lavatory, where it hangs with all the neighbors' tubs. It banged like thunder as I dragged it along the corridor, and somebody downstairs stopped snoring. But I finished the job, boiled a kettle in the kitchen, drew a bucketful of cold water, carried the lot into my room, bolted the door and stuck the key in the keyhole.

What pleasure it gave me to throw off my clothes, remove my wig, tear off my genuine India-rubber ears, and unbuckle the straps which constrict my back and chest. My body opened out like a potted palm brought home from the shop in wrapping paper. All the limbs which had grown numb in the course of the day came to tingling life.

I installed myself in the tub, seized a sponge in one hand to squeeze water over all the dry places, and held the kettle in my second hand. With my third hand I grasped a mug of cold water, added some hot to it, and tried it with my fourth and last remaining hand to see that it wasn't too hot. What comfort!

My skin freely absorbed the precious fluid pouring down on me from the enamel mug, and when the first pangs of hunger were allayed I decided to inspect myself closely, and wash off the unhealthy slime which had seeped out of my pores and congealed in some places in dry mauve clots. True, the eyes in my hands and feet, on the crown of my head and the nape of my neck were getting appreciably dimmer, from being covered up in the day time by rough clothes and false hair. The friction of my right shoe had

238

cost me the sight of one eye back in 1934. It wasn't easy to carry out a really thorough inspection.

But I swivelled my head, not limiting myself to a half-circle—the miserable 180 degrees allotted to the human neck—I blinked simultaneously all the eyes which were still intact, driving away fatigue and darkness, and I succeeded in viewing myself on all sides and from several different angles at once. What a fascinating sight it is, and what a pity that it is only accessible to me in the all-too-short hours of night. I only have to raise my hand and I can see myself from the ceiling, soaring and hovering over myself as it were. And at the same time I keep in view my lower parts, my back, my front, all the spreading branches of my body. If I hadn't been living in exile for thirty-two years I should probably never dream of admiring my exterior. But here I am the only example of that lost harmony and beauty which I call my homeland. What is there for me to do on this earth except delight in my person?

Yes, my rear hand is twisted by its permanent duty of representing a human hump. Yes, my fore hand is so maimed by the straps that two fingers have withered, and my old body has lost its former suppleness. I'm still beautiful for all that! Proportionate! Elegant! Whatever envious carpers may say.

These were my thoughts as I watered myself from the enamel mug, on the night when Kostritskaya took it into her head to murder me by means of a cracked bath. But by morning I was ill. I must have caught cold in the tub. The worst time in my life had begun.

For a week and a half I lay on my hard couch and felt myself drying up. I hadn't the strength to go along to the kitchen for water. My body, a tightly swaddled anthropoid sack, grew numb and inert. My desiccated skin cracked. I couldn't raise myself to slacken my wire-sharp bonds.

A week and a half went by and nobody came in.

I could imagine my neighbors joyfully ringing up the health center when I was dead. The district medical officer would come to certify the fatal outcome, would bend over my couch, cut open my clothing, my bandages and my straps with his surgical scissors, recoil in horror and give orders for my corpse to be delivered to the biggest and best of dissecting theaters as soon as possible.

Here it came—the jar of spirit, caustic as Kostritskaya's perfume! Into the toxic jar, into a glassy dungeon, into history—for the edification of posterity to the end of time they would plunge me, the monster, the greatest monster on earth.

I started groaning, quietly at first, then louder and louder, in hateful and indispensable human language. "Mama, mama, mama," I groaned, imitating the intonation of a tearful child and hoping to awaken the pity of anybody who heard me. And in those two hours, while I was calling for help, I vowed that if I lived I would keep my secret to the end, and not let this last vestige of my homeland, this beautiful body, fall into the hands of my enemies for them to rend and mock.

Veronica came in. She had obviously lost weight, and her eyes, purged of love and resentment, were serene and indifferent.

"Water!" I croaked.

"If you're ill," said Veronica, "you ought to get undressed and take your temperature. I'll call the doctor. They'll bleed you."

The doctor! Bleed me! Get undressed! Next she'd be touching my forehead, which was as cool as the air in the room, and feeling for my nonexistent pulse with her red-hot fingers. But Veronica only straightened the pillow, and snatched her hand away in disgust when it came into contact with my wig. Evidently my body only revolted her, like all other humans.

"Water! Water for Christ's sake!"

"Do you want it out of the tap or boiled?"

In the end she went out and came back with a decanter. She polished a dusty tumbler with such a pensive and leisurely air that I should have thought she was taking her revenge on me if I hadn't known that she knew nothing.

"You know, Andrei Kazimirovich, I really did love you. I realize that I loved you—how shall I put it—out of pity . . . Pity for a lonely, crippled human being, if you will forgive my frankness. But I loved you so much . . . didn't notice . . . physical blemishes . . . To me you were the handsomest man on earth, Andrei Kazimirovich . . . the most . . . man. And when you laughed at me so cruelly . . . make an end of myself . . . loved . . . won't conceal from you . . . worthy man . . . Fell in love . . . man . . . human . . . humanity . . . man to man . . ."

"Veronica Grigorievna," I interrupted, unable to bear it any longer, "please hurry. Water . . ."

"Human . . . manhu . . . hanumanu . . . Human . . . manhu . . . umanu . . . hanumanu . . . human . . ."

"Water! Water!"

Veronica filled the tumbler and suddenly raised it right to my mouth. My false teeth rattled on the glass, but I couldn't bring myself to take the liquid internally. I need watering from above, like a flower or an apple tree, not through my mouth.

"Drink, drink!" Veronica urged me. "I thought you wanted water . . ."

I pushed her off and struggled up into a sitting position, feeling like death. Water ran out of my mouth on to the couch. I managed to put out my hand and catch a few drops.

"Give me the flask and go away," I ordered with all the firmness I could muster. "Leave me in peace! I'll drink it myself."

Slow tears trickled from Veronica's eyes.

"Why do you hate me?" she asked. "What have I done to you? You were the one who didn't want my love, who rejected my pity . . . You're just vicious and nasty, Andrei Kazimirovich, you're a very bad man."

"Veronica, if you have so much as a grain of pity left in you, go away, I beg you, I implore you, go away, leave me alone."

She went out dejectedly. Then I unbuttoned my shirt and stuck the flask inside it, neck downwards.

Nature is all scurry and bustle. Everything is in a fever of excitement. Leaves come out hurriedly. Sparrows sing in broken snatches. Children hurry off to their

242

exams. Outside the voices of nannies are shrill and hysterical. The air has a tang in it. The Kostritskaya smell—in a low concentration—is all pervading. Even the cacti on my windowsill have a lemony aroma in the mornings. I mustn't forget to make Veronica a present of them before I leave.

I'm afraid my last illness has done for me. It hasn't just wrecked my body, it's crippled me spiritually as well. Strange desires come upon me at times. I feel an urge to go to the pictures. Or else I think I should like a game of draughts with Veronica Grigorievna's husband. He's said to be a first-class chess player.

I have reread my notes, and am not happy about them. The influence of an alien *milieu* is felt in every sentence. What good to anybody is this idle chatter in a local dialect? Another thing I mustn't forget before I leave—to burn them. I've no intention of showing them to people. And my own kind will never read them or hear anything about me. They'll never fly such an unearthly distance to this outlandish place.

It's getting harder and harder for me to recall the past. Only a few words of my native tongue have survived. I've even forgotten how to think as I used to, let alone read or write. I remember something beautiful, but what exactly it was I don't know.

Sometimes I fancy that I left children behind at home. Ever such bonny little cacti. Mustn't forget to give them to Veronica. They must be quite big now. Vasya's going to school. What am I saying, school! He must be a sturdy adult. He's gone in for engineering. And Masha is married.

Lord, oh Lord! I seem to be turning into a man!

No, it wasn't for this that I stood thirty-two years of suffering, and lay on a hard couch without water last winter. The only reason I got better was so that I could go and hide in some quiet spot and die without causing a sensation. That's the only way I can preserve what is left.

Everything is ready for my departure: my ticket and seat-reservation to Irkutsk, my can for water, a decent sum of money. I've got practically my whole pension for the winter on my savings book. I didn't spend anything on a fur coat, nor on trams or trolleybuses. I didn't go to the pictures once in all that time. And I gave up paying rent three months ago now. I've got 1,657 rubles altogether.

The day after tomorrow, when everybody's gone to bed, I shall leave the house unnoticed and take a taxi to the station. A hoot of the whistle—and that's the last you'll see of me. Forests, forests as green as my mother's body, will take me in and hide me.

I'll make it somehow or other. For part of the way I'll hire a boat. It's about 350 kilometers. And all by river. Water right beside me. Drench myself three times a day if I want to.

There was a hole. I'll search till I find it. The hole we made when we fell. Put wood all round it. Juniper blazes up like gunpowder. I'll sit down in the hole, untie myself and wait. Not a single human thought will I think, not a single word of alien speech will I utter.

When the first frosts begin and I see that the time is ripe—just one match will be enough. There will be nothing left of me.

But that's a long time off. There will be many warm and pleasant nights. And many stars in the summer sky. Which one of them? . . . Who knows? I will gaze at them all, together and individually, gaze with all my eyes. One of them is mine.

Oh native land! PKHENTS! GOGRY TUZHEROSKIP! I am coming back to you. GOGRY! GOGRY! GOGRY! TUZHEROSKIP! TUZHEROSKIP! BONJOUR! GUTENABEND! TUZHEROSKIP! BU-BU-BU! MIAOW, MIAOW! PKHENTS!

1966